AF397421

Pinar Akdag

Wisdom from the heart

novum pro

© 2022 novum publishing

ISBN 978-3-99131-532-2
Cover photos: Absentanna, Anna Poguliaeva | Dreamstime.com
Cover design, layout & typesetting: novum publishing

www.novumpublishing.com

"I believe that every great religion,
be it Judaism, Christianity, Islam, Hinduism or Buddhism,
can lead to perfection, enlightenment, and salvation.
I believe in freedom, equality, brotherhood, peace, and human rights.
And I believe, despite all the obstacles on earth, that man is noble, precious, and heir to virtues.
All those in the world who choose goodness and seek perfection are my sisters and brothers.
This work is dedicated to all those who are 'seekers' in life."

In the name of the good, the sublime, the righteous, the virtuous, the perfect …

… let this book be dedicated to Him, the Creator of worlds …

… May this book be a support in the life of the reader and give him strength and courage; may it provide the reader with new ways of thinking and occasions to think, so that it contributes in a small way to alleviating discord on earth …

Contents

1. Kuvvet and the Sage

A young woman named Kuvvet had searched for truths all her life. She collected precious knowledge from all corners of the world and delved into her faith, Islam, to find answers to her questions.

And then the time was ripe.
The student was ready.
And she met the Sage, who recognized the illuminated being in Kuvvet.
So the Sage decided to teach her truth and wisdom.
And so began the teaching that would pave the way for Kuvvet.

The Swamp

Kuvvet and the Sage were talking.
Again and again, the Sage paused, smiling as he sank into thought.
"You remind me of someone."
She looked at him quizzically. "Who do I remind you of?"
"Would you like to hear a story?"
"Sure."
"I'll tell you about him."
Kuvvet nodded. "I'll listen."
The Sage began.
The story was about someone who had awakened.
"Long ago, when life was less complicated, but just as turbulent as it is now (if not more turbulent and dangerous), there lived a little boy. He was a very ordinary boy. Every now and then he would get certain thoughts stuck in his head and ponder the meaning of things, but being so young, inexperienced, and a bit indifferent, he just as quickly shook them off and went about the life of an ordinary boy.

What the child did not know was that he was actually asleep. But still he grew. He became more mature. He learned and thought. He thought about all sorts of things. He thought about everything you *could* think about. He was seized by a thirst for knowledge. It was as if he were possessed. He wanted to learn more, to know more, to soak up everything there was to know about God and the world. He became a man. And one day this man woke up. What he saw when he woke almost drove him mad. He was not in the world he had thought he was in. Instead, he was up to his waist in a swamp. Strangely, his torso was smeared with muck. Something or someone must have pulled him halfway out of the mire while he was asleep. Incredulous and confused, he looked around him. And he received another shock. All about, people were up to their necks in the slime. Their eyes were covered with colored glasses, and earplugs were in their ears. Any time one of these earplugs fell out or the glasses slipped when they stirred, the implement's owner would immediately shriek in fright until some shadowy figures came and silenced him with a swift kick, replaced the device, and disappeared.

The man was on the verge of despair. He saw everything clearly now, but he was still trapped, held fast in the mire. He began to thrash about, desperate to get out of the bog, tugging with all his might. This only ensnared him more tightly and dangerously in a tangle of vines about his legs. To make matters worse, the beasts who lived in the brackish arrived. Animals he could scarcely see began to bite and scratch him. Panicked, he screamed for help, but to no avail.

After a time, he began to think: something or someone had pulled him halfway out of the mire to see if he was worthy of assistance. This meant that he had to get out of his predicament on his own. He had been pondering this a long time and had almost reached the end of his mental and physical resources when he suddenly had an idea. The dangerous, venomous swamp animals had been at him, and the strange, devilish figures had later joined them. They were all attacking him now, trying to maneuver him back down into the mud, already certain of victory. But the man kept smiling calmly. He had changed his strategy.

Do you know what he did? He stopped doing anything. He let his exhausted legs, still stuck fast despite all his efforts, rest. He ignored the enraged vermin. He let the shadowy figures hovering above the water continue to pummel him, paying them no mind. For every pain he suffered, he imagined one day being free, receiving his just reward, coming face to face with the invisible helper who had pulled him this far out of the foul, putrid waters. An incredible desire took possession of him, just as it had before. At last he knew, at last he understood, what was really happening around him. At first he was very happy, but also very naive. He firmly believed that he could save all of the others. So he began to snatch the glasses from those nearest him and to pull out their earplugs. But he had not anticipated the second way in which these people had been trapped: They had been made to forget that they possessed a heart. They saw the truth, but did not accept it. They squeezed their eyes tight shut, pressed their fingers firmly into their ears, and began to scream at the top of their lungs until the beings responsible for maintaining their stupor came and replaced their blinders, releasing them from their torment.

So he stopped trying to help them and focused once again on his path through the ocean of swamp. As time passed, he grew older, wiser, and stronger, and became relentless. The beasts and demons rarely ceased tormenting him, but often a helping hand intervened to drive them off, giving him a brief respite. In these moments, he half-recovered and bowed in deep gratitude to his helper. And sometimes he felt a warm, delicate breeze pass by, touching him sweetly and cooling his deep, burning wounds. He knew that someone was trying to encourage him, urging him not to give up. Because if he did, he would soon start sinking into the mud again. That must not happen!

With enormous longing and love, he kept raising his head, just when he was about to give up, with a fierce determination. He stared straight into the eyes of the devils as if to say that he would no longer be intimidated. With calm, steady movements, he searched his immediate surroundings for solid, reliable objects such as rocks jutting out of the water or large plants that he could use to carefully pull himself forward. How often he was at the point of drowning, but how often he found a shallower path on which he could even proceed quite comfortably. His mood fluctuated wildly. Sometimes he felt like an angel, free and happy, and sometimes he was ruthlessly brought back down to earth. And again and again he continued on his way.

Because he wanted to prove to his helper that he was strong enough to get out of the mire. He would make it. That much he knew. It all took his breath away because, as the mature man he had become, he realized how infinitely beautiful, perfect, unique, and all-encompassing the unknown helper was … and how much greater that beauty must be even than his imagination could conjure up. He had to see him! He had to find him. Somehow.

Sometimes he didn't want to stop speaking to him for very love, and sometimes he bowed his head in shame because of his guilt and wickedness. And again and again he whispered to his helper that he did not want to give up; it was only for him, for this longing for him, that he wanted to endure the sufferings of the swamp, to be enveloped one day by his love forever and ever …"

The Bubble

Kuvvet and the Sage were talking.

And as the conversation drew to a close, the Sage fell silent and looked warmly at Kuvvet.

"Whenever I see you lately, Kuvvet, I am reminded of one of my old stories."

"What story do you mean?"

"It is a story about a very special soap bubble."

Kuvvet looked puzzled. "A story about a soap bubble?"

The Sage nodded gently. "Would you like to hear it?"

"Yes. Gladly."

"Then I will tell it to you."

And the Sage began.

It was the story about the progress of being.

"Once there was a beautiful, shining soap bubble.

It delighted observers and made them smile.

The bubble thought that it was its beauty and unique appearance that pleased them. But it was its purity and need for protection that touched people's hearts.

The bubble learned this from a visitor, but did not yet understand completely.

The bubble grew older.

And its own brilliance and purity diminished. It dipped more and more often into the soapy water and one day realized that the soapy water had all been used up.

So the soap bubble went in search of more.

It soon found a mud puddle.

'I must dive in here if I want to survive,' it thought to itself sadly.

Someone happened by at that moment and spoke soothingly to the bubble.

'We humans, too, must often suffer and overcome burning seas if we are to survive.'

'Thank you!' the soap bubble called out to the passerby.

And it jumped into the puddle.

When it emerged, it was a muddy ball. The mud soon dried, and the bubble looked at itself. 'By overcoming that, I have obtained a firmer shell. I am no longer as fragile as I once was.'

And the passerby said, "Now you are different from ordinary soap bubbles. The Creator has granted you a second skin of earth for better protection from the dangers that surround you.

Among humans, too, many have thicker skins which they acquire through suffering and pain.

But there is a secret to this stronger skin.'

'What kind of a secret?'

'Come with me,' the wanderer advised.

And they returned to the other soap bubbles.

The bubbles floated in front of their soapy water, delighting onlookers.

When they saw the ball, they greeted it.

The ball was confused.

'They still think I am a simple soap bubble.'

'They haven't come as far as you have, so they don't know. They perceive only as much as their eyes can see. It is the same with people.

They perceive what their eyes see and recognize only what they themselves are.'

The ball thanked his companion and continued its travels.

It soon came to a new realization: 'I have a firmer shell, it's true, but I am still hollow inside.'

And the ball collected flowers, grass, wood, and rock. And it filled the space inside it.

Soon it felt full enough and went on.

It again encountered its friend, who could see the change in the ball.

He said, 'You have now acquired inner abundance and security. We humans do that by gaining knowledge and accumulating life experience. This gives us more certainty and steadfastness in our being.

And the ball continued on its way.

It thought to itself, 'I am reaching maturity. But believing I had already reached it would be immature. I am a ball. Some are and remain simple soap bubbles. Most are. Others, like me, have more solid shells. We recognize each other immediately. But they do not see my inner fullness.
They see only as far as they themselves have come.
Then I encounter soap bubbles that have equally solid shells and are full inside.
We recognize each other.
And today I know that there are also balls that are further along than I am. They shine when I see them. I do not understand where their glow comes from.
I can see only as far as I myself have come.'
And as the ball went along, it began to think.
All its maturity had not yet made it glow.
The most important thing was missing.
And it thought, "I am unique. Why is that? I think. How can I do that without help? Or is it without help? Do I have help? Has someone created me and brought me this far? Who was it? How do I find him?'
Again someone came by and listened to its suffering, smiling approvingly.
'You seek the Creator, little ball. He has hardened your shell, given you a rich inner life, and led you to Himself.'
The ball thanked him and asked to hear more about how to serve the Creator.
And little by little, it began to shine.
'So now I have come to the end of my wanderings. I need no more.'
And I tell you, Kuvvet:
Good is heaviness imposed by the Creator. It is necessary heaviness. But forced, self-imposed heaviness is foolish.
What the Creator gave you, good or bad, ultimately became good for you.
What you took upon yourself, if it was good, became good.
And what you took upon yourself, if it was bad, became bad for you."

Teach Me How to Cry

Kuvvet and the Sage were talking.
Soon a man came by, empty and full at the same time.
He asked for their attention, and they gave it to him.
He said, "I want to learn to cry. Whatever I do, I can shed no tears."
The Sage watched him carefully.
"Learn to feel."
The desperate man murmured, "I do feel, I do. I have felt so many things. So many feelings have raged in this body."
"Then suffer."
The stranger pressed his fist against his chest, "My heart has almost burst with pain."
Now the Sage understood.
"So love and warmth are missing."
The man looked up in amazement. "What is love? Is there anything like that anymore?"
Then the Sage looked at Kuvvet.
A meaningful glance passed between them.
Kuvvet said:
"What we allow to be taken from us we can take back again. What is torn from us we can reconquer together when we have become stronger."
And the Sage said:
"Man fades away and perishes when he lacks love
Suffering without love is like the smoke of a fire.
It dwindles, and there are no flames to spread and burn.
Feeling without love is like spring without the sun.
Nature does not bring forth its splendor.
Living without love is like living without air.
The flowing blood is empty and no longer brings life to the organs.
So seek love, poor friend from whom it has been snatched away —
by others or by himself."

Wistfully, the man looked up.

"Where do I find it?"

Sadly, the Sage rubbed the stranger's shoulder. "Within yourself."

"I can't find it there."

The Sage fell silent for a moment and thoughtfully pointed at the man's heart, where love had expired.

"This heart must return to life once again."

"How can it do that?"

"It must thaw and escape its icy prison."

"Show me how."

Smiling, the Sage now began to recite from the Koran.

And the stranger cried. He cried as though his heart were breaking.

And then he emitted soul-refreshing gusts of laughter.

"The Koran?" the stranger asked.

"Allah's book. Yes."

Full of new life, the man stood up, determined.

"I have suffered a great deal. I had to become hard. So now I want to learn from Allah to become human again.

He gives me value.

He will not leave me alone or abandoned.

I want to be human again.

Authentic people are still so rare.

So let me become human again.

Thank you.

And now I will be off to seek bliss.

And now I will drink the glistening water of sublimity.

Farewell and be certain that I am not so easily buried in the fire's embers.

I just needed a brief ray of hope.

Peace with Allah has been breathed into me.

I will find myself again.

And henceforth all my sorrow shall fade away."

The Path of Man's Life

Kuvvet and the Sage were talking.

The Sage asked, "Do you know the path of a man's life?"

Kuvvet shook her head. The Sage raised his hand and began his instruction.

"Man goes through life on a path as thin as a hair, but as firm and unbreakable as iron.

In the course of his life, he learns to walk along this path with some degree of confidence.

If a gust of wind comes, he may lose his balance.

If the thread vibrates, he may lose his balance.

If a storm comes up, he may lose his balance.

If there is rain or ice, he may lose his balance.

And whenever he loses his balance, he suffers.

Illness, pain, suffering, misfortune, grief, and much more … anything life can inflict.

Each person is allotted a path by the Creator, a path he is able to travel.

Very many have a relatively harmless path ahead of them.

But if a raging storm comes, they may fall from their path.

And once they fall, it is almost impossible for them to find their way back.

It's hard to recover.

Then there are those that are shaken violently from the beginning.

They learn that they must sometimes cling to their paths not only with their feet, but also with their hands.

And when a big thunderstorm comes, they do not fall from their path.

They are tough.

And what about true believers?

Here, too, there are different life paths.

But when a storm tests them, they know that they must not give up the hope of better times.

They know that the Creator gives suffering to those with strong backs.

They know that the Creator gives only as much suffering as a person is capable of bearing.

They patiently hold out until better times come.

They learn to fight, with themselves and with the world.

And they know that the Creator will reward them for their effort.

No matter what path the believer has taken, is taking, or will take, he can never give up if he holds fast to these basic ideas.

He will not give up hope or the will to win.

But some never get used to the narrow path of life because they have not gone through any serious difficulties.

And others become acrobats because they have undergone serious training.

They know that their path is a game that tests their endurance.

At the end of the path, they will be either rewarded or punished. And you yourself know why."

Kuvvet nodded. "Depending on whether I chose the good or the evil path. Because every now and then there are forks in the road, and I have to choose between the better and the worse path."

"Very true. So be prudent in your actions and always travel toward the light."

Kuvvet smiled. "Where else? Could I live or breathe without the light? It has become my reason for living."

The Sage laughed warmly. "What would you say about those whose purpose in life is this narrow path? Surprising as it may sound, that's how it is with many, many people. And they will realize their folly only in the hereafter."

Where We Stand

Kuvvet and the Sage were walking past a mountain.

The Sage pointed to it and said to Kuvvet, "Tell me, where do you think man stands?"

Kuvvet replied quickly, "At the top ..." But then she looked up in confusion.

"... or in the middle ... or way down at the bottom." She looked at the Sage. "Tell me, where does man really stand?"

The Sage laughed. "He is at the very top ... and also at the very bottom." He folded his hands behind his back and looked toward the mountain, shaking his head slightly.

"The Creator made man the highest creature and at the same time the lowest. You can overtake even the angels or measure your worth against a mosquito. It depends on just one thing: who your friend and companion is. If you hold fast to the Creator, you can rise to great heights, but if the devil is your friend, you are close to losing everything of value, and you stand alone in the other realm on the way to the lake of fire. Those who are close to the Creator will be rewarded eternally in Paradise. And you should know that you will get only what you have taken upon yourself and deserved. There will be no injustice there."

Kuvvet pointed to the mountain. "And what if man were to be in the middle?"

The Sage smiled. "Most people are basically good, but they commit many sins. They commit them from weakness, incorrigibility, or folly.

There are few truly good ones.

And few truly evil ones. Ordinary people are between good and evil.

And they should always turn to good and try to keep evil away.

And remember: Only prayer to the Creator and gratitude to Him can satiate and satisfy your soul and heart. For your soul needs nourishment just as your body does.
So immerse yourself in paying homage to your Creator."

The Pearl

The Sage instructed Kuvvet:
"Know, Kuvvet, that every person possesses a pearl.
At the same time, there are two kinds of people, differing in the way they handle that pearl … but there are actually three kinds of people, and it is precisely the precious third kind that is still extremely rare today."
Kuvvet thought about these words for a moment, then said, "I would like to hear the wisdom behind this teaching in more detail."
The Sage looked up briefly, then gazed into the distance before replying, "Today, most people let the pearl gather dust, failing to recognize its value.
Others put the pearl on an incredibly intricate brooch.
Now consider the two pearls.
Neither remains what it once was.
The one treatment diminishes the pearl's value, or so the owner thinks.
The other is intended to give the pearl its deserved place.
But neither owner notices that the pearl remains what it is.
The one considers his pearl musty and outdated.
The other finds it blindingly magnificent.
Neither sees the pearl for what it is. The third group tries to accept the pearl as it is: pure, true, and honorable – the greatest virtue and goodness.
They care for and honor the pearl, taking it with them everywhere as a companion. This is the noble approach.
The pearl in its natural form has become rare, Kuvvet … it is either misunderstood or most grandiosely idolized.
But the pearl aspires neither to death nor to arrogance. It is simple and pure, a treasure in itself.
Why do people not simply leave it as it is?
It cannot be made invisible.

And the more you presume to add to its splendor, the more you alienate the breathtaking splendor of its true nature.

Thus, Kuvvet, you must learn to maintain a delicate balance when handling this precious pearl and simply let it be as it is.

For dust on the pearl cannot take away its value.

And no rigid pomp can express its true value.

The pearl alone – no matter what people without knowledge and understanding do with it – is of inestimable value.

… And the Creator will one day judge us all according to how true and rightful our handling of the pearl has been. This fundamental responsibility is certainly not a burden that everyone can bear."

The Telescope

The Sage said to Kuvvet, "Did you know that there is a telescope that can make the light of the Creator visible?"
Kuvvet shook her head. The Sage returned a pained smile.
"I would not have expected you to.
Only a few people know about this telescope.
Most people are content with the nourishment their predecessors put before them.
People still talk about eternal light today.
But no one is looking for it.
Because no one believes any longer that there are miracles and light in life. They all think that those times are long gone. They think that the incredible is hidden and extremely rare.
This telescope has been forgotten."
Kuvvet thought about that. "We should tell people about it. That would give them proof of the Creator's eternal being, after all."
The Sage frowned slightly and shook his head. "Unfortunately, we can't. If you showed people the telescope today, they would see nothing in it.
This telescope has a secret: It is very, very large and separated into shafts.
Fundamentally, each person has such a telescope.
But most allow it to gather dust, since they have forgotten about it.
If you do know about the telescope, you try to set the shafts evenly so that the telescope provides a clear view of the light.
Some shafts are biases blocking the view.
Others are fellow human beings, the environment, and the influences they exert.
Many other shafts are each individual's own gross errors.
Some shafts are the devil, urges, ignorance, vices, and much more.
The greatest people are those who manage to catch a small ray of light from their telescope.

But has anyone ever managed to see the light completely through his telescope? The Creator alone knows.

We, on the other hand, should worry only about using the telescope. May the Creator guide our hearts in our endeavors and show us the path that leads to Him."

Life and Death

Kuvvet and the Sage were watching the sun set.

For a long time, the Sage watched with dignity and gravity. At last he began to speak.

"Do you see the light that reaches us and the red that surrounds the sun?"

"Yes."

The Sage smiled. "This is a brief truth that reaches us.

The light is eternity. The red is transient.

The soul is eternal. Blood is mortal."

Kuvvet looked at him quizzically. "What about the other colors? Surely they too have meaning."

The Sage nodded. "Imagine a rainbow. It is a message. It goes from red to yellow to green. This is nature: the grass, the leaves on the trees, and the flowers. They are the closest to life. Then comes blue: the oceans, the seas, the lakes. They are in the fourth position."

Kuvvet smiled. "Is there more?"

The Sage nodded. "What is missing?"

"Black."

"The Creator made life from the darkness. The green plant grows from the black earth. What do we see from this?"

Kuvvet stared at an invisible point in front of her.

"The rainbow that appears against the gray-black clouds. The fire that leaves behind black ashes." The answer was within reach, and finally she had her epiphany.

"Black stands for death. Colors stand for life. Each receives from the other the power it needs to exist, which means …" She looked up at the Sage in amazement.

"… that which is above is eternal. It draws the life force from itself."

The Sage now raised a hand to stop her. "That is all that is proper for us to discuss.
The Creator is without beginning and without end.
This is the truth that requires no further proof."

Knowledge

Kuvvet and the Sage walked thoughtfully along the trail through the spacious valley, stopping to admire a large meadow with knee-high plants growing wild as the wind swayed them gently. The Sage gazed quietly at this peaceful landscape and then looked out into the distance. He spoke pensively to Kuvvet.

"There is a something very precious … knowledge.

Knowledge is salvation. Knowledge is healing. Knowledge is liberation from suffering and pain.

You can obtain knowledge by seeking the truth, reflecting, and trying to understand existence.

Learn – learn throughout your life, Kuvvet.

Educate yourself in all the things you are passionate about.

Without education, your path will be far more difficult.

The more knowledge you have, the easier it will be for you to progress in life.

Learn about the world; learn to be what you are capable of learning about.

This will enable you to understand more and to patiently heal your soul, step by step.

Always try to anticipate what whoever may be facing you is thinking.

Don't leave the thinking to others. That is where danger lies. Remember that."

A Bird

Kuvvet asked the Sage a question:
"Tell me, how do I appear to you?"
"Like a bird."
"A bird?"
A smile played around his lips. "Yes, a bird. To understand that, you must know that a bird can be caged. You can clutch a bird tightly, preventing it from spreading its wings and rising from the earth. But you can't expect it to take root if you bury it in the ground. Of course not. The bird would dig itself out and take to the skies once again, no matter how many times you bring it back down and try to discipline it. It will know how to free itself each time and fly back into the sky."

The Blade of Grass

Kuvvet and the Sage were standing in the middle of a meadow. Gently Kuvvet knelt down and picked a daisy and a blade of grass. She presented them to the Sage

Smiling, Kuvvet sat down, lowered her head, and propped her chin on her arms, which were folded over her knees, and gazed ahead.

"I don't think of myself as a flower. I am a blade of grass. I may not be as ornate, and I may not be a decoration to nature." She gestured towards the landscape.

"But just look. A simple blade of grass, to which we assign so little value, is so beautiful when joined with its peers. It is the green that enlivens our souls and comforts us.

Of course the flowers attract more attention. But how beautiful would they be against an arid landscape?

It is the same with the leaves on the trees. It may be that which seems worthless that is of greatest value.

No. Don't let me be a flower.

Let me be life."

The Sage raised the hand in which he held the plants.

"Don't Muslims compare the Prophet Muhammad, may he rest in peace, to a rose? What do you say to that?"

"The Prophet lived the life of a blade of grass. He reiterated this over and over. He spurned riches and led a simple life. Only those around him made the comparison to which you refer. They believed the rose was the correct analogy. Is that enough for you?"

The Sage shook his head. "That is not the whole truth."

She thought for a moment and smiled.

"Maybe he was a rose after all. But that rose lived like a blade of grass."

The compass

The Sage said to Kuvvet, "Dust off your compass. Breathe life into it again."
Kuvvet thought for a moment. "I'm not sure I understand what you mean."
The Sage smiled gently. "Knowledge, ideas, and internalized truth will help you bring your compass out of darkness of ignorance. Then it will always guide you.
You are responsible to the Creator for yourself only – whatever you do, good or bad, for yourself or others.
But this doesn't mean that you should orient your life completely towards the outside.
Be good, be safe.
But turn inward to yourself.
If you wanted to satisfy the world, whether it were good or not so good, you would lose yourself.
Return to yourself and do not get lost in the maze of opinions and expectations.
You, too, are the work of the Creator.
You, too, possess a compass.
Do not listen to those who say, 'Do this, do that' – those who command you.
Listen to those who give you advice, and always consider for yourself whether what you are doing is right.
Learn to understand existence and internalize truths from everywhere so that your compass will start to work again and you awaken from your sleep."

The Bond with Allah

One evening, the Sage spoke to Kuvvet about the bond with Allah. "The bond with Allah is unbreakable. The bond with Allah is your heart.

Your heart is your compass in existence. And your compass is an extremely sensitive network of pure feelings, knowledge, understanding, and insight that you must form reliably over time. If you sincerely use your heart and do not turn outward to the world to be tossed about by it and torn in all directions, but listen to your heart, the compass, you will not perish and lose yourself. No matter what kind of chaos surrounds you, your compass will guide you. Let your heart, your center, which is love for Allah and reverence for Him, guide you.

Then nothing can break your bond with Allah."

2. Kuvvet

A desire arose in Kuvvet.
She yearned to seek for maturity and wisdom.
She revealed her wish to the Sage.
He was delighted.
He said, "You seek completion.
My advice to you is this:
Live with your eyes open.
Think about and hold on to what you have found.
Let your faith in Allah be your companion and guide.
Go, Kuvvet. Go and fight for Allah."
Kuvvet remained silent for a while. Then she silently bowed her head and said, "I go, dear Sage. My quest will be eternal."
Kuvvet did as she had been told. Together we will see what happened to her and what she learned.

The Singer

While she was walking one evening, Kuvvet heard loud music coming from the open window of a nearby house.
She stopped and listened, spellbound by the melody and painful lyrics.
"Who is it that suffers so greatly?" And she went into her home and sat down.
"So let me enter into his spirit and let him speak."

"I need love," the young man said.
"No matter what I did, my innermost being was consumed with genuine love.
I searched.
Everywhere.
I sometimes found love briefly.
But I wanted enduring love.
And I searched.
Everywhere.
But it was so strange.
Once I loved without fear and doubt.
My heart was broken. A woman broke it.
I wrote odes, poems, and songs about my pain.
I shouted my suffering!
I wept for my invisible, streaming blood!
I was discovered.
I was made a singer of the modern age.
Those who surrounded me were superficial.
They wanted to be near my success.
I remained alone.
I remained alone!
Why?
Why did I remain alone?

I needed love.
Only heat.
Why am I being left alone here?
I fell in love once again.
She loved my success.
When she saw me, the man in pain, she just laughed and walked
away.
I was naked!
Where should I go?
Tell me, someone, where should I go?
My pain makes me more successful!
My songs have great melodies!
Where can I find friends?
Where can I find compassion?
What do you all want?
Do you want me to become stone?
Who is pressuring me?
I was looking for love.
I lost hope.
So I took what they wanted to give me.
My friends were the whiskey bottle, superficial flesh next to me
in bed, and the inner abyss.
The abyss stayed there when they left me alone.
Who do you think I am?
Tell me! Who?
Is your order good? Is my chaos bad?
All I wanted was love.
All I wanted was love!
I often smashed my furniture.
They brought to me new furniture.
And the worse I got, the more successful I became.
Blank faces cheered me.
Again and again.
I could see only the silhouettes.
All I wanted was love.
But I got no love.

I was drowning in money.
Designer clothes.
Luxury cars.
Expensive jewelry.
Beautiful women who lusted after me.
I was envied.
So many were hostile to me.
Then hate me!
Hate me!
I do not hate you.
Do what you want.
Go ahead, do it.
Then one day I was standing in front of the mirror.
While I stared at myself, the mirror shattered into tiny splinters.
It was as if time had suddenly become viscous.
I saw almost all the shards, millions of them, detached from the whole, regaining their breath, breathing perhaps for the first time.
They shouted thanks and farewell to what was once the whole and went their way.
My face was rigid.
Now I saw only the bare wall in front of me.
My head lowered mechanically, me scarcely aware of it.
Golden sunlight flooded the bathroom.
Diamonds glowed.
And the red of my blood that flowed onto those broken pieces in the sink did not stain them.
No one would ever again look into the mirror now that the shards had become self-aware.
Now I saw rubies and diamonds, sparkling courage to me.
What did these creatures, normally the aftermath of destruction, mean?
They had not been destroyed at all.
But we like to judge according to our own conceptions.
It was just that a new form, a new type, a new existence had emerged.
Whether we like it or not.

And then I saw something shining on some of the pieces.
What was it?
The light was almost sacred.
Who are you?
I no longer understood my heart.
It emitted the most peculiar rhythms.
What is wrong, my heart?
Slowly I raised my bloody hand, examining it curiously. Detecting a slight tremor, I let it rest on my chest.
Be calm, my heart.
Everything is all right.
Everything is fine.
Then I felt metal.
My heart gave a painful leap.
All surfaces, corners, edges, and colors began to fade.
Do what you think best.
I reached for that piece of metal.
It was my cross.
I lowered myself to the floor and took off that chain.
It was as if I was seeing it for the first time.
God. And Jesus.
Yes. I am a Christian.
Christian?
I am a Christian.
I wanted love that much?
For the first time in my life, I prayed consciously and from my heart.
Tears ran down like threads, dripping onto my torso.
My Lord is here. God, you are here.
Protect me.
I can't go on.
I am suffocating.
My Creator!
Will you give me love?
Can I trust you?
I broke down.

And God was with me.
He gave me strength.
I had never been taught to believe properly.
I found Him by myself.
In great need.
The Lord is great.
He's been my everything ever since."

Kuvvet said, "Listen!
Who knows who is like you when you are like everyone else?
Maybe you are just a dying breed of person that has become rare?
One among hundreds or thousands who want what they have,
but not you?
Who is going to find you?
Tell me! Who besides the Creator?
And on it went until the mirror had to crack."

Rewards and punishments

Kuvvet went for a walk one day in a quiet village.

As she moved toward the nearby valley, she saw a young woman praying to the Creator in despair and unhappiness.

Kuvvet heard her words as she passed.

"Lord, please make this pain and suffering end. Lord, I can't bear it, it's all so hard."

Kuvvet gazed silently at the young woman as she stood under a large tree looking up at the sky and finally decided to approach her. She listened attentively to the young woman's expressions of grief and stayed with her silently for a long time, sharing her suffering and comforting her.

When the young woman had finished, Kuvvet smiled gently, was quiet for a while, then spoke earnestly.

"What you did not realize, good woman, is that you were forcing a solution.

You did not accept the suffering, instead regarding it as torment and torture.

You rejected the idea of exercising patience. After all the years of temperate living, a little testing upset you completely.

You thought suffering a punishment and therefore completely unjust.

So hear me:

There are two kinds of suffering. For the ignorant and unbelieving, it is a punishment.

It is a punishment because they do not believe in a Creator. This is because they are not initiated into the deeper truths of faith. And since they do not know about these deeper truths, suffering constrains them.

After all, they believe only in life on earth, or else they are indifferent to existence. And so they wish for nothing more than a nice, fulfilled earthly life, with happiness and health, for as long as possible.

Unbelievers and the ignorant organize their lives according to coincidence and do everything in their power to have things go well for them on earth.

Now, when they encounter suffering, whose severity lies in different concerns for each individual, they feel punished.

Listen: The Creator alone knows what constitutes suffering for you. You may not fear fire, but there will always be something that you find difficult to bear, and that is your personal fire. Suppose Allah let someone suffer a severe affliction: that is how the unbeliever and ignorant person suffer. No matter how he sees it, he will receive ill fortune with reluctance and distress.

He always wanted everything to be good and perfect, but that was not always possible.

So he was often dissatisfied, and when he began to suffer, his unbelief deepened.

The more ignorant experiences he had, the less he wanted to search for the truth and was instead confirmed in his ignorance and unbelief.

But he did not know the truth.

To know it, he would have had to seek it.

And to seek the truth, he would have to be a truth-lover.

And to love the truth, he would have to be truthful.

Now listen to me carefully, for I am explaining how a believer deals with suffering.

Misfortune is not always easy to bear, even for a believer.

But he knows that both good and evil come from the Lord of the Worlds to test people and separate the righteous from the wrongdoers.

The world is, after all, the testing ground for human beings.

Bad and the evil enable you to distinguish the good and the right from it and teach you to show sincere gratitude for this good and recognize its value when it is gone.

Suffering teaches the believer to struggle and strive and to endure earnestly and patiently. For he hopes thereby to pass this test in the eyes of Allah and to attain a better rank before Him and win His favor.

Likewise, he sometimes draws sustenance from suffering like a holy wine that strengthens him, steels him, and makes him wiser and more sublime.

Believers see suffering as a gift from Allah to the servants He especially values, since great rewards await them when they overcome it. The Lord also burdens those who can bear much, so never give up.

'I will conquer suffering and become worthy of the Lord or die trying,' says the believer.

He looks for solutions, for ways of making the suffering bearable, or he searches diligently for answers.

For he knows that Allah has left him to his own test, and he will not let anyone take that test away from him. The believer wants to prove himself to Allah and show Him how much he can fight and what burdens he can bear.

After all, he lives only once, and even if the world knows nothing of all the struggles of his inner world, Allah knows every detail. Nothing else matters.

He does not ask for suffering, but accepts the trials Allah sends without complaint.

He burns, blazing brightly, but the fire is not laced with dissatisfaction and impotence, but with a heat from the depths of the soul. He fights, he hopes, he waits, he suffers sublimely, and the inner fire inspires him.

He loves the Creator and hopes and longs for the good that may soon come to him.

More and more he immerses himself in this surging sea of flames and pays no attention to the injuries that befall him.

In the end, the fire of faith, this endless longing and love for Allah, is so great that the burning of suffering is sometimes a satisfaction that almost cools the ever-present heat of faith.

While he is dealing with the suffering, he can show Allah in small steps how much he loves Him and how gladly he jumps into the flames for his love, time after time.

You must know that believers do not live a moderate life inside. Even when everything seems orderly and temperate outwardly, inwardly they are waging sublime, precious, and legendary battles and experiencing the most tremendous and radiant extremes, which transport them to paradisiacal spheres even during their earthly life."

How to Speak to the Sunset

Kuvvet was in her room.

After she had eaten, she got up, washed her hands and face, and went to the bookcase to inspect it more closely. After a few minutes, she realized that she didn't want to read any of the many books today, and crossed to the window, where she opened the shutters fully and took a deep breath. The sun had already set, and the scorching heat had given way to a pleasant, fresh summer air. As the light disappeared and darkness took possession of the land, the landscape around Kuvvet became stranger and more mystical. The mountain that commanded almost her entire field of vision looked like a black wall. The light emanating from behind it seemed to come from another realm, as if salvation and paradise, consisting only of warm, soft colors, sounds, and scents, were waiting there. A few miles away, it invited them to leave this hard, cool world. Longingly, she lowered her head and felt the wind blow past her into the room.

"Why? What is it all for? What is it all for? It's all meaningless. It's all so weak, so worthless, so pitiful, so bad, so gloomy, so blind, so deaf, so lifeless, so joyless …"

She raised her head again and looked up. Finding no bright spot in the firmament, she murmured her weariness.

"I will probably never reach this realm. It escapes my grasp again and again. It greets me, entices me, and before I quite understand what is happening, it is gone again. Why do you do that? To seduce other people the same way? Will you also show them your most beautiful side, beguile them too? Make them fall in love with you? Then leave them standing in the dark, lonely and abandoned? Why are you so heartless? So ruthless? How can you still find pleasure in this game? Or is that what you are here for? To give us hope for our life after this one? For so long you have been pursuing your destiny … and I? What about me?"

She was wracked by a soundless laugh. She alighted from the sill and stood upright.

"I am and remain a human being. I can't help it. I give up again and again, then continue with my tasks, stumble, injure myself, shed tears, bleed, tend to the wound that will add to the rest of my scars, get up again, find a beautiful flower, rejoice, and press on, only to encounter, at the very next corner, something else oppressive, unpleasant, and difficult to bear. Yes, I am just a human being. Thank you, sun. Thank you, sky. Press on. Continue in the paths the Lord has marked out for you. You do not know our fears. You do not weary. You just drift. Do what you have been told. Do you sleep? Always? Are you dreaming your endless dream? Can you even hear me? Even if you can't … thank you. And you, great mountain? You seem so mighty, so huge, so sublime. Wouldn't you, who have only to exist eternally, be brought low by our burden? I don't think you could not bear it at all. Would you crumble to dust? To you, too, I offer my thanks. Thank you."

Now she felt good again, strong again. It didn't matter if she was mistaken, if she was fooling herself. She thought her truth. She needed no more truth than that.

So she stayed where she was, content to gaze into the deep night in the dark room and watch the twinkling stars as a silent admirer. It was incredible. She, a human being, was so insignificant. But these stars in the firmament, which were actually enormous planets, seemed so tiny to her. How could it be, how was it possible, that a simple human being could rise again and again to the sky, and fail again and again out of arrogance and hubris, sometimes brutally. Sometimes, far too often, he put himself in mortal danger

"It's just part of us, after all. Isn't it, you beautiful diamonds that silently look down on us? I think I know what you're thinking. Or did you whisper it to me? A few short words, scnt to me fleetingly? I know, I know. We came after you and will leave before you. A human life is nothing. The earth must suffer much at our hands. You feel for it, don't you? But you also tell it that

the guests on this blue planet will soon be gone. A great, exalted hand will call the curtain down on the play. And then settle
accounts. On that day, everyone will account for their actions.
Let them beat their heads against the wall, follow their senseless
ways. Soon it will all be over."

The Ant

Kuvvet noticed something moving on the floor. On closer inspection, she saw that it was an ant.

"What do we have here?" She bent down and let the ant crawl onto her hand. Then she got up and went out into the garden. She knelt down again and deposited the ant on a blade of grass.

"Little friend, I must admit, I didn't used to value to your kind much. And I valued myself even less." Resting her chin on her folded arms, she contemplated the insects crawling around.

"Little ant, I am watching you. I am watching you in your tireless work. I see your efforts and your will to live and build. Don't you know that a careless step by us great creatures could destroy you and your laborious work? Your home would be lost.

And yet you would start your work all over again. And again. Because surviving is your goal. Providing for posterity is your aspiration. And believing in the future is your disposition.

Little ant, who gave you this disposition? Was it by chance? By what coincidence did you achieve these complicated structures? What coincidence gave me my mind? And what coincidence gave us our will to live and survive? Who gave the mother her love for her offspring? Who gave the father the strength to protect and care for his family? And who brought us into being?

Know, little friend, that it was not by chance.

It was the Creator. Only the Creator. The sole Ruler of the worlds. Little ant, He sees you at night on the dark ground, just as He sees me in my search for truth. And He cares for and watches us both. Just like this butterfly fluttering past me. He knows us all. He knows what is inside us as well as what we show on the outside. We cannot hide anything from him.

Little ant, do you know what the Creator is like? Do you want me to explain it to you? Do you want to know?

The Creator exists. He is self-sufficient. He depends on no one, but everyone needs Him. He has no beginning and no end. He sees everything, He hears everything, and He knows everything. Finally, He bequeathed to us humans a small part of His all-encompassing knowledge.

Are you wondering what the Creator looks like? I don't know what He looks like either, little friend. We are not supposed to know here on earth. If we were to see Him during our trial here, everyone would believe in Him. But not everyone should believe. Only those who want to find Him should believe in Him. For this is how He will determine who deserves to be close to Him in the eternal life that follows death.

Little ant, I know only that He is holy light. That is all I want to know in this life. It is enough for me. As long as I may think of Him, I am satisfied.

You know, you and I are not alone together. There are three beings here. And if we were in a group of ten, eleven beings would be present. If the group were a hundred, one hundred and one would be present. Because the Creator is also there. He is never absent. He neither eats nor sleeps. He possesses all perfection, and all defects and faults are far from Him. And to you and me He gave the honor of knowing Him. What more do we need? Little ant, what do you think? Tell me."

And the ant paused in its work and looked at Kuvvet.

"I believe in the Creator. Every creature does. Only you human beings are different. You vary in faith. Some believe, some do not. That is how it should be. That is how it must be. On earth, you humans have an opportunity to prove yourselves to the Creator. Some do prove themselves. Others do not."

Kuvvet stared ahead, cocking her head to one side. "Doesn't He want everyone to believe?"

"Without the bad, there would be no good. And everyone decides for himself which path to take. The test of life is just so hard that only some will pass it."

"And what is the test of life?"

"You are to seek and find the Creator and live a proper, good life. In spite of all the difficulties that may stand in the way."

"How am I supposed to know what's good and what's bad?"

"That you will learn with the bright knowledge of the world and with the help of your heart. And now I must return to my duties. After all, I want to do justice to the role the Creator gave me. Farewell. Allah's blessings be upon you." She smiled.

"And on you. May the Creator give you what is best."

Where Are You?

In the spring, Kuvvet walked along a narrow footpath through a lush green valley, looking about her.

"Lord, where are you?" she whispered.

Then she raised her head and looked at the bright clouds that left wide white trails like foam on waves.

"You are everywhere," she said.

She lowered her gaze and looked at the loose pebbles that on the path.

"Who are you?

You are the One who created heaven and earth and everything in between and put us human beings here to face the test of life. Where did you come from?

You never came. You were always there. You are from eternity. Without beginning and without end.

Where did I come from?

I came from You. I will remain here on earth a short while, then appear before You.

What am I for?

I am to be a servant to You and to live my life accordingly. Everything I do, I do for You to obtain Your mercy. I am on earth to undergo the test of life and to train myself for eternity.

Why am I suffering?

I have my life in my hands. Much of the evil is my own fault. Some of it is a test. And by experiencing both the bad and the good, I am maturing and becoming an individual. This strengthens and shapes me and makes me a human being.

What am I?

I am a human being. And a human being is animal, angel, and devil in one. What you allow and what you refuse is up to you. You also choose which of the three has precedence. You and you alone choose who to succumb to and who to triumph over.

What is the world?

It is the scene of human deeds. It is the place where humans are tested.

What is life?

It is a game. It is a challenge. And it is the sphere of opportunities. Only in life can you prove yourself or lose yourself. There will be no such opportunity when life is over. Then people will say either that you won or that you lost.

What is after death?

Death is the precursor to eternal life, real life. Remember: Your time in this life is as short as drawing a breath.

Who will go to paradise?

Those who demonstrate their belief in a Creator in what they say and in what their heart says, and who practice doing good for Him.

Does it matter what you believe in?

No. Who you believe in is not the main thing. The important thing is believing in a perfect Creator and in the good in existence."

Kuvvet looked up and blinked.

Once again, she had let herself be carried away by her thoughts. She shook her head, smiled, and went on.

"Is it so hard to believe in one God?"

But what does it mean to believe? Who has time for such questions? The world is dreary and will remain dreary. People are entangled in their lives and hardly have time to look up. So they have no opportunity to deal with the details of existence.

The Stars

A woman approached Kuvvet one day and shared her thoughts. "Surely any person could become like the saints were, if only they made an effort."

Kuvvet smiled and shook her head firmly. "The saints, as you call them, are like the stars.

They illuminate the world at dark hours.

People, on the other hand, are like the darkness around the stars.

They are never able to shine – that's the province of stars."

The woman pondered for a moment. "What is the reason for this difference?"

Kuvvet looked at the woman. "It is because of the degree to which the light of omnipotence has been internalized."

The woman thanked her and left.

Kuvvet looked after her. Her eyes glowed softly until a mist veiled her endless inner fire once more.

She sighed longingly and whispered imperceptibly to herself.

"And it is because of how much the truth has penetrated your being, how much you have been overcome by truths whose longing filled you, how much you have understood your existence, how much you have internalized the bright treasures, and how much you have adorned your soul with true treasures.

The ornaments of your soul were basically what made you shine.

But tell me, good woman, in your world, what truths remain? Where should I start explaining, and where should I stop? We are worlds apart.

I am not saying that one of us is better than the other.

What I want to say is this: What has become of mankind? And why is my kind so unworldly today and why … why does nobody know the truth anymore?

Each person leans on the one in front of him.

Everyone seems content with his existence.

The world is well-decorated … but the body often is not.
We have enough to eat and live contentedly.
But are all souls happy? Or do we instead console ourselves with the decorated world?
Yes, the world is beautiful.
But, good lady, many, many souls today are deserts without life.
Dusty and dry, drought pervades the souls in this world."
Kuvvet gazed earnestly ahead of her.
"It is time for the truths to return once again to the consciousness of mankind."
Kuvvet's sad face gradually gave way to a smile. She continued walking, gazing into the distance.
"It is time for the stars of today to find each other. Humanity should learn how to see them again and discover their endless silence, which confronts the immoderate world."

The Robin

Clouds covered the sunny meadow with soft shadows, and birds and crickets sang, each in his own language, rejoicing in the beautiful expanses surrounding them, following life with their courting instincts.

Kuvvet entered this scene tentatively and sat down on a rotten tree trunk.

She took a deep breath and tried to relieve her depressed inner self.

She looked around, humming softly. Then she began to speak:

"Those who do not wish to hear profound truths, but rejoice when the topic is the world … there are so many of them.

That depresses me.

Those who have suffered misfortune suddenly call upon the Creator for assistance.

That amazes me.

Those who think they are fighting in Allah's name, but go too far and cause destruction and untold suffering, surround us.

This weighs on me.

But there are those who still truly believe and labor in the Creator's name.

That warms me."

She looked around her.

"It seems that today everyone has to decide for himself where he stands. More than ever before."

A robin flew down and touched the ground in front of Kuvvet. It said, "Always and everywhere, man has had to decide for himself. It's just that today it is no longer that easy to lean on the person in front of you. Because today you know not only your neighbors. Today you know the world. And there is much turmoil in it. And your race, in its struggles with one another, needs more honesty, which you find hard to accept."

Kuvvet agreed. "But what should we do?"

"From that madness, light will shine, and you will find what you seek."

Kuvvet smiled. "The world revolves around every single person after all, doesn't it?"

"Certainly."

"Then those individual worlds should consist of more than just this world. Doesn't the Creator have the right to enter human life as well?

It's time for the people to understand."

The robin nodded soberly. "They will. They will. For some, though, this will happen after the test here in this world is over."

Kuvvet stood up. "Then we should try to reach some."

"That's right."

They said goodbye and admitted the greatness of the world and the repetition of their journey.

Talk to the Tree

It was a foggy day.

Kuvvet walked slowly through the land, absorbing the dreamy sights.

"Land that passes me by, how I adore you. How I long for complete harmony with you."

She paused in her wandering and looked at a peculiar tree.

It held her gaze.

She smiled.

"Do you want my friendship?"

She walked up to this tree and touched its thick trunk.

"What wisdom will you give me? How can I always remember you, so that I can call you my friend from now on?

There are moments when my strength fades. And then, deep down, I am tempted to say, 'I can't go on. I give up.' But, proud tree, I immediately resist this temptation. What I actually say is, 'I do not give up. Things will continue. They will.'" Warmly she looked at the whole tree.

She whispered.

"Now what do you say to this poor girl?"

And she listened.

"Remain upright. Remain upright. Remain upright. If you fall, do it with your last breath. Otherwise, remain upright. If you are wounded, mourn that wound quietly. If you are exposed to stormy weather, don't be afraid to tremble. When you are exposed to the cold, remain reserved. But do not lose your upright posture."

She glowed inside. "Thank you, tree."

Kuvvet lowered her head cheerfully, scanning the leafy ground with its yellowing grass, and rose with a composed expression.

Having learned this, she now left her friend.

She raised her hand and pointed at the landscape around her.

"You, earth, are my friend. I am always seeing new sides of you. I like you very much. Teach me throughout my life. When I part from one thing of beauty, the next one comes. Thank you, my friend."

Burning Seas

A woman came to Kuvvet with a request.
"It is said that the best of the best had to overcome seas of burning fire.
But today, and in the past as well, many have done that."
Kuvvet smiled and shook her head firmly. "No, they haven't."
The woman looked at Kuvvet in surprise and asked why she said that.
Kuvvet inhaled longingly, remained silent for a while, and then explained, "A burning sea makes you holy, insignificant, or bad. A burning sea is something that everyone has to cross in smaller or larger stretches of life.
But this is not just about crossing a burning sea.
It is about trying to be a true human being in spite of every burn, the agony, the torment.
You think to yourself that you would like to suffer, but you want no distasteful suffering or suffering that is unpleasant for you.
But the secret of the burning sea is that it contains everything bad and base as well.
If you cross these seas and keep your light, then you are one of the true crossers. Then you have truly crossed burning seas.
This is not simply a matter of making it across a burning sea and surviving without paying attention to whether you have gathered much darkness within yourself afterwards.
This is about going into battle against darkness firmly anchored to the light."

To the Creator

One day, when Kuvvet's wandering on earth again went to her heart, she began to pray to the Creator. With sad eyes, she whispered, "What if I asked you, Lord? What if I asked you to bring some light back to this dark world, Lord? Return it to peace, Lord? Finally stop the incessantly flowing blood, Lord?
I miss you, Lord
You leave us to ourselves.
And we fail, Lord.
Some want property.
Others want revenge.
Some want power.
Others want to share in it.
Some are abandoned.
Others are blinded.
And you watch us in our existence.
For we do not call on you, Lord.
But that won't always be the case.
The time of faith will come again.
What else is there for us, Lord?
I am always searching. For the good, the pure.
Where did it go?
We have gone astray. Long ago. It is gloomy here, Lord.
We need you. Do not leave us alone. We are lost without you.
I beg you, Lord: Save those who turn to you. Save those who need you.
Especially in these days that are gloomier and gloomier, do not leave us alone.
And you will not leave us alone. For you are the Merciful One, the Righteous One.
We will wait patiently for your signs.

And they will come.
And we will be victorious.
And we will heal.
Amen."

Probability

A middle-aged woman sought out Kuvvet and approached her:
"I want to believe.
But doubt often gnaws at my will.
Tell me, Kuvvet, what can help me carry my faith with me safely?"
Kuvvet nodded kindly and said, "Clear, watchful, eyes; an open, understanding ear; a devout, honest mind; and a kind, warm heart will keep your faith strong.
And just look at the world and the universe:
Everything is in eternal order, and nothing is out of place. Look at everything in our existence and ask yourself: What is wrong here? Nothing. Nothing is missing.
Everything follows a law: the planets, the plants, the animals, and our own physical bodies.
Now tell me, what is the probability for everything in existence to be so perfectly aligned? Without a deficiency or flaw?
To err is human, that is true.
But that is because humans go through trials.
Some will pass the test; others will not.
And if you are able to give me an answer, if you say that the world came from nothing to achieve perfect order and cite a certain probability, I still ask:
A work of art does not arise spontaneously, you say.
Then what about the artwork called existence?"

The Dream

One night Kuvvet had a dream that she would never forget.

She lay on a lush green meadow, looking up at the sky.

But just as she was starting to get tired of looking at its endless depths, her parents appeared in her field of vision.

Kuvvet looked at them. Yes, her parents had been her role models for many years.

Her parents smiled blissfully at her and stepped aside.

She saw what was behind them.

There stood the Sage. And yes, he was Kuvvet's greatest support and a venerable role model.

The sage smiled at her, then he, too, stepped aside.

And Kuvvet continued to look.

There now stood the Prophet Muhammad. Kuvvet's eyes were fixed on this majestic image. The greatest of all her role models now stood before her.

But he smiled at her and stepped aside as well.

Kuvvet now saw the universe.

And she floated up, in complete harmony with being.

And she cried, "Free! Now I am free after all! Only the Creator stands before me.

The Creator alone is my eternal companion.

Everything and everyone are friends. I learn from the great, bright personalities of the world.

But I am no longer able to follow silently.

Yes. I too stand today at a place where it would no longer be right to follow a person. I now have too many of my own views after years of learning and following. What every person should seek and attain is to learn from everyone and be willing to understand and internalize that knowledge.

You, man, are as unique as your views on God and the world. Do not argue. **Speak** and learn. Learn and read and learn again. Think, understand, and internalize. Step by step.
Give me a truth that convinces me, and I will accept it. For I am a seeker. And seekers absorb everything in order to grow, to satisfy their souls, and to better understand.
Learn from everyone. And then learn from yourself.
And the Creator invites me to strive for Him.
So I go … for all that matters is the Creator alone."

The Streetlight

A woman out for a stroll spotted Kuvvet standing on the green summer roadside, touching the top of a streetlight that was lying on the ground.

Curious, she came closer and asked what Kuvvet was doing.

Kuvvet looked up pensively.

"I used to see this streetlight rising so high into the air. As a child, I wished I could touch its highest point.

And today this old streetlight lies before me, and without effort, I can stand here and touch the top. Before, it seemed so unspeakably difficult."

The woman nodded, bade her farewell, and left.

Kuvvet thought, "If it is arranged by men, the top of what is achievable may be at the bottom tomorrow.

What you strive for today may be something everyone succeeds at tomorrow.

What was at the top of the list yesterday may be commonplace today.

So why bother trying to live up to expectations?

Why not search for your own highest ideal?

This is more important and pleasant to me than the crazy competition out there."

3. From Kuvvet

Kuvvet had learned a great deal from the Sage.
And she had experienced a great deal herself later.
Then she had thought a great deal about God and the world.
So Kuvvet decided to write down what she had thought and discovered.
For understanding minds and truth-loving souls.

The Ice

A green land with flowing streams, full of life.
This is how the elders talk about the past.
Then came the winter.
And would not go away again.
Little by little it conquered life and did not rest until everything was buried under the ice.
With heavy, pounding steps, the few survivors sometimes wandered through the countryside, looking around.
They saw people, encased in ice, living a cold life.
Were they still people?
Their hearts had stopped beating.
They had been frozen long ago.
Instead, they allowed themselves to be steered by circumstances.
They did what was necessary in an almost human way.
Only their eyes betrayed them.
Their eyes were empty and betrayed the absence of hearts.
And something strange was going on.
They were trying to surround themselves with even more ice.
What had killed them had now become their purpose in life.
And so, the living strode on.
They saw young people on the verge of giving up.
They sought to warm each other by partying, throwing themselves at each other, and losing themselves in dancing to loud music.
And they didn't notice that they were disappearing faster as a result.
They would soon gradually enter the icy world.
There was no escape.
And an adolescent boy sat alone on a roadside in the semi-darkness.
His shoulders were slumped, his face hidden behind the arms folded over his knees.
When he exhaled, his warm breath made a cloud.

Then he lifted his head, looked up wearily, threw the beer bottle away, and paused.

His heart gave a painful leap.

This did not frighten him.

It had happened a few times before.

It was only a matter of time before he would give up.

Not quite as imperceptibly as others, but at least it would be quiet.

He would freeze into ice and thus finally be able to live with less pain.

His lips pursed, and tears started from his sad eyes, becoming crystals even before they reached the snow.

He took the next bottle of beer and brought it to his mouth, but it had been outside too long.

The liquid had solidified.

No panic crept up inside him.

A strange calm entered his mind.

Everything suddenly seemed so insignificant.

He slumped, then lay on the path with his limbs outstretched, laughing softly as much as his numb body would allow.

He closed his eyes.

He could hardly feel his hands or feet.

"This is how I let myself go.

It's better this way.

Before I am forced to surrender.

Before I am forced to serve the ice."

He felt as if the life were slowly draining out of his body.

"Is this my soul?

I feel it so intensely now.

I wasn't able to give you much, soul.

Can you hear me?

But I am still myself.

I'm still me."

And he fell asleep.

And those who still lived came along.

One of the men looked down at the boy.

He wrapped his arm around the boy's neck, straightened him up
a bit, and poured him some warm tea.
The boy came to, blinking.
The man asked him, "Do you want to live?"
"I want to be truly alive."
"Then I'll take you with us." Once again, the boy lost consciousness.
When he came to again, he was in a warm place.
"How can it be so warm?" he asked the people in the room.
"There are ways of generating heat," said a voice, and the man
who had rescued him appeared.
"How do you feel? You've been out for a long time."
The boy sat up. "I'm all right." And he looked around the room.
Then he saw a book that radiated light and warmth. The man
noticed the boy's amazement.
"This is the Holy Book. It protects us from the eternal ice."
"The cold can't get it?"
"No, it can't."
"So, there is no perpetual ice."

Years passed.
The boy fought against the ice. With his friends, he freed those
not yet lost. He grew up.
All the living gathered to him.
And each one pressed his Holy Book against his chest and advanced.
And after many battles, the snow began to melt.
People fled to those who had the Holy Book.
And one day they saw the sun.
And soon they saw grass.
And soon they heard birds chirping.
Humanity awakened.
And the man who had once almost succumbed to the ice cried
out, "The Creator will not let the world perish as long as there
is one believer! We trusted Him to liberate us! The time is ripe.
To Him we are devoted. Allahu akbar. Allah is great."
He kissed his book.

"We ourselves were to blame for our situation! And behold! He still freed us! It is Him we must serve … Elhamdülillah. Praise be to Allah." He took some of the snow that still lay on the ground and clenched his hand into a fist from which water dripped.

"Don't you see? Cold is not equal to man! We cannot live with it, and it cannot coexist with us! We were close to succumbing to it! We almost became its subjects! No. Not believers. We resisted, even when we couldn't force it back. The Creator saved us … Subhanallah. Allah is far from all shortcomings and faults."

And a bird flew over the people.

It alighted before the believers.

It chirped.

"The Creator. The one God." And the young man looked up to heaven and stretched out his arms.

"The Creator will always be victorious. Go, bird, and proclaim this in other countries that do not know us. The Creator will always be victorious. And so will those who stand with Him. No matter the circumstances. The Creator gives victory."

A tear trickled down his cheek and fell onto the snow.

The snow melted where it fell.

And he looked up and went on to seek out other lands.

And he whispered.

"Bow down to the truth only.

Then the lie will kneel before you."

Come Down

"I see you.
You saw that ladder and began to climb.
Some struggle to find those ladders.
Some are handed them.
And others find them on their life's journey.
The paths to get to them are different.
But the result is the same:
You climb up into vastness that remains hidden from others.
And soon other people seem so unspeakably small.
And you feel so big.
Come down, friend.
Come back down, friend.
Just come back down, friend.
Why doesn't a person become a giant when he develops, achieves, or completes things?
Because this is not in his nature.
It's just that suddenly, whether you want it or not, that ladder is there in front of you.
It does not make you bigger, better, wiser.
It just allows you to climb.
I get dizzy so quickly at great heights.
It may be more dangerous than on earth, where you actually live.
Don't you know what happened to those who fell down there?
And how lonely it may be up there?
Are you calling me to come to you?
I think about it first, and then grasp the rung with my hand.
I reach you at a dizzying height.
And you sit there before me, looking up at the stars.
Your face is so peaceful."
"I've gotten further than others," you whisper.
"I don't like it here," I say.

"Why?" you ask.

"These heights are no friend to life," I whisper.

"Come down to where your life path awaits you. At these heights, you have forgotten where you come from," I tell you.

"But I'm one of those who belongs here," you say.

"No," I reply.

"You yourself must not climb or cause yourself to rise to great heights.

Hearts may lift you up, arms may raise your images in the air, and you may be carried, but does that make it right for you to take the first ladder you find and try to become something better? And to climb higher than you deserve?

Only the Creator knows who you really are. And His judgment is the only one that counts.

Stay on the ground, whoever you are."

And we climb down in peace.

"And who knows," I say.

"Perhaps the Creator will raise you in the other realm

So, work towards it and approach Him only."

But then I look at you.

Now you start digging.

"What are you doing?" I ask.

"Now I want to be the most humble," you say.

I stop you.

"This is just as bad as the other," I say.

You drive the shovel into the ground and ask me what is to be done.

"Take the middle path. Stay on ground," I say.

"Doesn't everyone take the middle path?" you ask.

"No," I say.

"They follow their life. They know only the earthly way.

But the few among them who know the middle path and take it are exalted, and you can recognize them immediately. You see their struggle flashing in their faces.

So, do not climb into the air, and do not dig into the ground.

Always take the middle path," I advise.

"But I feel I am different from ordinary people. How can I turn my innermost self toward the outside?" you ask.

"By living the faith and practicing patience.

And be content with things as they are.

For you see, in order to progress and prove yourself, you may have to overcome seas of fire.

Would you take that pain upon yourself?

Would you take upon yourself seemingly unending suffering and torment?"

"No, I wouldn't," you think.

"Realize, then, that you get just as much as you deserve.

And know that every person thinks he is special or wishes he were.

And see that every person is special. But it is not you who reveal your true greatness, but those who recognize you."

And you now stop short and begin to smile.

And you rise from the earth.

I see you floating, with mild surprise.

You take me by the hand, and together we rise into the air.

"What if I can fly?" you ask.

"I have nothing more to answer. You seem to have true greatness in you," I say.

"So there are bigger people after all?" you ask.

"Yes," I say.

"Those who have inner greatness," I say.

And you fly down again to earth.

"Whether I have greatness or not makes no difference to me now. I choose the middle path and hide the way I am. I will think uniquely and present myself as ordinary people do," you say.

"Those like me will recognize you," I answer.

"And those like me will recognize you," you say.

"What will you recognize?" I ask.

You smile.

"You too can fly. Your hair is blown by the wind. And you have lived in the depths, trying to be the humblest person, until you found the middle path. You are full of earth, don't you see? And you have spared me all these troubles and given me advice.

And my advice to you is this:
Seek the middle path in everything, but every now and then you should still fly or dig.
Because you want to live greatness, not the ordinariness," you say.
"Then hear me!" I say.
"It is the middle path that challenges those like us.
Take the middle path, but you will always live and find greatness.
And fly and dig only when no one sees you.
If you were to show others your greatness, you would become smaller than would please you.
Greatness is something you carry in your heart, not on the outside.
There is a reason for this, don't you realize?
So, learn to maintain balance.
And learn to keep silence.
And think and learn much.
And fight and endure much.
So that greatness is formed and grows in you.
This is for those who are looking for greatness.
And serve and love the Creator only.
This is for those who seek the love of the Creator.
It is all they want.
But they are the greatest.
For the greatest are those who do not see or want to see their own greatness."

The Wings

I have wings.
They are made of flames.
These are there for a reason:
I myself am on fire. My innermost being glows and sends bright flames through my shoulder blades.
My body could no longer hide the inner fire.
For years I burned without anyone noticing.
My blood boiled, my bones burned, and my self was heated.
And at some point, when it became unbearable, it happened.
I crumpled on the floor in pain, my arms wrapped around my knees.
I trembled because of a tremendous wave of flame, and when there was no more room in this fragile body, fire shot out of my back.
Now bystanders could see my agony.
I could no longer hide it.
But the bystanders felt threatened by the fire.
And I myself did not want to harm anyone, so I fled to solitude.
This saddened me.
"Why doesn't your fire go out?" asked the fire.
And it said, "You are different."
I said, "But only because you don't let go of me. Everyone thinks I am different and ill."
And it said, "Don't you see?"
"What?" I asked.
It said, "I gave you wings."
And then I rose from the earth.
Like the wind I flew through the countryside.
Overwhelmed, I thought: Only further … let me fly further.
The fire said, "There is a reason why the fire has taken such complete possession of you."

"And what might that be?" I asked.

"You feel so much pain," it said.

"That is certainly true," I replied.

It said, "Do you want to know how to achieve more tolerable warmth so that you no longer burn?"

"I do," I exclaimed.

"Even though you can fly now?" it asked.

I looked up earnestly and landed on a deserted beach. I spoke urgently now.

"All my life I have been different. My type was rare, and few understood me. And now, these days, I am entirely alone."

The fire said, "Isn't it good to be different? Is it perhaps even a great gift and a mercy?"

I considered that.

"You do not know my pain. You are the one who scorches me. I am the one who suffers."

The fire said, "Cover your chest with your wings of flame."

I did as I was told.

It was as if I was being covered and wrapped up, and a comfortable warmth now reigned within me.

The voice of the flames sounded softly, "Longing for truth is what burns within you and has come to surround you.

This fire is sacred.

It shapes and steels you.

It keeps you awake.

And it keeps you from forgetting."

I said, "The torments I suffer are to keep me upright on my path and strengthen me?"

It whispered, "Yes … yes, yes, yes … yes, yes …"

And it said, "And know that if you were to reach your goal, our fire would go out. Today you are pitied, but tomorrow might be completely different. Know again that you will always be fighting something. And you will rest purified only until the ncxt wave reaches you."

I rose from the earth and flew to great heights until I noticed a gleam in the distance.

I flew towards it.

Soon it blinded me, and I could no longer look at it.

But I kept flying toward the shining light.

And soon I reached it.

It spoke to me

"You found me.

Fewer and fewer people find me.

Fewer and fewer people visit me.

Fewer and fewer people recognize me.

Do you know who I am?"

"No," I admitted.

It said, "I am faith in the Creator."

"So faith in the Creator is what I was looking for," I said.

"Yes. And you are different from those who reached me before," it said.

"Why?" I asked.

The radiance gently passed over me.

"You shall now know," it said.

"What am I to know?" I asked.

"It is light that is in you and around you," it said.

Then a deafening noise arose, and the fire transformed into warm light.

I couldn't believe it.

"I suffered and burned for faith?" I asked.

"Yes. You would not have found it otherwise. If things had been otherwise, you would have quickly turned back and perished with the world," it said.

I embraced the rays and said farewell:

"I have done little. I have suffered much.

My fears were mortal. My longing and search were eternal.

I am small. My Creator is great."

Today, it is difficult to enter the path of truth.

But the Creator's reward awaits you at the destination.

Only those who are prepared to burn can take that path.

So tell me: Who has courage?

Tell me: Who is strong?

Tell me: Who is fearless?
And I see you setting out.
Farewell.
Let your heroism be a witness to the modern age.

Passionate Burning

"I burn, suffer, and rage.

This is my elemental passion!" The words echoed from the blazing forest.

"I spread out as far as I can, encompass the world in my clutches! Everything is mine, everything must belong to me! Everyone must recognize that I fill out even smallest corners with my gigantic fullness!"

These words resounded from radiant, flickering, flowing, raging masses of flames. The mighty fire burned, destroying the land and the trembling forest.

"I have no consideration for weak life, for my fulfillment drives my urge. And my fulfillment is the passion, the searing love in my innermost being; it must expand and encompass everything. Too great is my longing to reach the highest heights and remotest shores!"

The enormous sea of flames thus had no mercy and grew into a destructive monster.

But then it stopped short, hearing a familiar sound.

Pleading and shouting reached its ears.

There was a campfire far away.

In the dark, it recognized its relative in the distance.

"Stop, reckless, insatiable wildfire. Do you want to destroy these innocent forests? Must they perish for you? Will you extinguish pure life, the forests and flowers and animals? Will you ruin this fine world simply for your vanity? Stop then, for otherwise you will be one of the unjust!"

The sea of flames paused briefly, then flared angrily.

"Since time immemorial, it has been the fire's nature to burn until everything is in ruins. The more it eats, the more it hungers! Speak no further, for I seek to act according to my being! Insatiable, full of abundance!"

The campfire now spoke forcefully.

"Do you not see that passion, unbridled and without light limits, only destroys? Has your mind become clouded? Have you abandoned all temperance and clear discernment? No matter what you do, it brings only harm. You have no more utility. Everything excessive will cause harm. Where is your virtue? Do you have the right to use destruction in pursuit of your goals, to destroy the forests? Is it good to be arrogant and to view others as worthless and superfluous? Is it not up to the Creator to decide life and death? Are you not acting as though you were a god, and will that not result in eternal loss? And even if you were divine, why would you cause only death and destruction when you are supposed to sow life?

Look at me: I am equally full of passion, yet I respect my boundaries. I am here, under control and full of utility. I give warmth to the people and thus even keep them alive.

Don't you know that extreme cold and extreme heat destroys them? Pleasant, mild warmth revives them. That's how they use me and prepare their food.

Yes, in a way, human beings also possess a burning fire within them.

They call it love and passion.

In healthy quantities, this fire inspires them to work wonders. Anything excessive destroys them."

The great sea of flames was about to laugh in derision when rescuers appeared to attack the destroyer.

Little by little, the wildfire lost strength and became smaller.

Then, in desperate fear, it called out to the campfire.

"It seems the times of destructive, death-dealing passions have come to an end. The people have found a way to end my ravaging here. You were right, campfire made by human hands.

I see that I will disappear from the earth.

But I realized in time that in this world, restless passion in primal form is scarcely possible anymore. But listen: I am and remain passion. I had no evil intentions. But what you said was true: I have no right to impose suffering and torment on others.

But I have found a way to survive thanks to you, my friend: I don't want to be a campfire. That would constrict me too much. I want to burn on to all eternity. And for this, I choose the wise man. After this failure, my being will pass on to noble people, keeping them upright during the testing period of their lives on earth.

For in truth, my passion was for one Person only: the Creator alone. Love for Him scorched my understanding. Tell me, was I a hopeless fool to be so reckless and violent, unable to see because of searing love?

Then let me enter into the breasts of the pure, the wise, the gifted. They will have trouble breathing, of course. They will tremble at the waves of flame and burning and experience an inner death … but no matter what happens, they will firmly embrace me and keep their passions from deteriorating into error.

No, passions will inspire those who are good.

They will reject evil, fight wickedness, and shun what is sinful. And they will run towards Pure Virtue, fighting for it and defending it.

Henceforth, let my fire burn in these people and inspire them on earth, keeping them upright on the path that leads to Allah alone."

And as the last flames of the wildfire died down, it spoke its last words:

"O my Creator, I was completely blinded by endless love for You. Forgive this fool and fulfill his last wish, O my Creator."

The industrious people had done it. The wildfire was extinguished. They rejoiced greatly and mourned the forest that had been destroyed.

Suddenly a brilliant light enveloped the place, lifting itself into the air and flying away, sparkling, in all directions.

The campfire, which had been mourning wildfire, its foolish relative, was now merry.

"Your wish is now fulfilled, you poor wildfire. You had too much power on earth and caused only destruction. But enter now into the bodies of the good.

You will accompany them in struggle after struggle, and they will grow in and with you.

Always remind them, especially now that people are in such danger of forgetting, that Allah alone counts. For Him we will gladly fight and suffer."

The Silent Breast

In the depths of the dark night, a dazzlingly bright light was born. But the light did not ascend to illuminate the earth. It did not accept the obvious as its home.

After all, the light had not come from the original light and did not follow any predetermined paths.

It had been created by the venerable Creator from the primordial being, from the eternal silence, the nothingness, the weightlessness, the bottomless depth.

A silent man, yet so fond of wallowing in the endless expanses of his heavy breast, drew from the all-encompassing ocean, found this fine, clear light, and accepted its request:

"Take me into your breast, which has always struggled meekly with itself and with the worlds, not often openly, but secretly, in a place where hardly anyone finds their way. Where battles rage and breathe life into the world.

Place me in the most secret corner of your heart, where no living being can enter.

Let me take root there and grow with you.

Receive me and call me a part of you.

Receive me and learn to know the truth and understand it with wisdom and courage.

Receive me, and you will find your path, sooner or later. It will not be far off.

Then, when you have received me, you enter into a holy covenant: You will burn. Longing will fill you completely.

You will search. You will embark on eternal wandering.

You will suffer. But light sufferings are beautiful and strengthen you from your very core.

You will love. A divine love, an elemental trust and a powerful support will grasp you.

Once you have absorbed me into your still gloomy breast, which suffers in the dark night and yet does not stop fighting, you will have a friend and helper in time of need.

And if your trial on earth is still so difficult, bliss from such a deep, endless source will fill you and never ebb away.

Many things in life then want to lure you to them and beguile you.

I will pull you back then, back to me. Do you think that I will let go of you?

Do you think that you are no longer a part of me? And do you really think my endless love will depart from you?

Understand, beloved, you are too precious to me to disappear into oblivion.

You have fought thus far. I am now your reward. And I will always take you to me when you forget yourself.

When you forget who you really are.

When you forget how holy you are.

For oh, beloved, you are longing.

You are the delicate breath of the omnipresent, omniscient, omnipotent, perfect Creator.

You! For you are the governor on earth, to testify who you are. Be good, always choose the right, and strive with heart and soul for the good.

And even if no one perceives what burns in your breast and how much you struggle with your radiant light, remember:

The Creator sees everything, whether open or secret.

Never give up.

The Creator is with us.

And I, your light, will always be your companion."

And the struggling man soon became a hero, a saint, and a legend. And the world? Painful as it is, it did not get to know that man. He went his lonely way in the gray, noisy world. He was secretly the warrior of light. And he left all reward to the Lord of worlds. And the world remained upright thanks to that hidden treasure of the Divine. And all reward and truth about that silent warrior and other heroes fighting all over the world became apparent and manifest at the entrance to real existence:

At the beginning of eternal existence.

Then the Lord of the worlds will bring everything out into the open:

What was in your deeds? What was in your intentions and your goals? And what was in your breast and your heart?

Did you choose the light or the night?

Or did you get lost somewhere in between?

Did you choose eternal victory or endless defeat?

Did you choose the Creator or damnation?

Nobody forces you to do anything.

Not even the Creator.

In life, you decide.

Then, in eternity, the Creator chooses.

Go. The light is ready at any time, until the end of your earthly test. You alone will decide.

May the Creator be with you.

The Fire

A fire once broke out in a country.
It blazed up, growing with dangerous rapidity.
Soon this land was called "scorching heat".
And the inhabitants of that land were led to the fire.
"Come to me and gain power," said the deep red flames.
And the people came.
Those who opposed this dangerous unity were expelled and isolated, and those who fought against it were exterminated.
"Follow me and rise above others," the embers exulted.
And the people gathered into one big unit.
Soon, because they were blinded, simple-mindedness grew in the masses.
The desire to survive and be superior was all that remained.
Each wanted to surpass the other, so that the people would fall in line to kiss the fire's burning hand.
And soon they were just fire as well.
After all, skin cannot resist the heat for long and melts away.
The heart loses its will and bursts.
The mind wants power and opens itself.
Power.
Give me more power.
Abundance.
Give me more abundance.
The fire discovered a swarm of bees.
It fought on against the enemy.
"You possess something that I want," murmured the sea of flames.
And it took the golden honey from the bees.
"This is our existence! Stop! You have no right to do that!" the hard-working insects shouted.
But the fire took what it wanted.
It took everything from those who did not submit to it.

Those who resisted were robbed of all their possessions.

"It is your turn at last," the fire said.

Many gave up.

Only a handful remained.

"No!" they shouted.

"There is still hope for us. The Creator will save us."

The fire laughed.

"I have been rampaging so long. And still your Master has not stopped me.

I do as I please with you, and yet it is I who am rewarded.

So tell me: where is your God?"

With the last of their strength, the freemen stood erect.

"The Lord leaves you unmolested so that you may do more mischief, entangling yourself deeper in guilt.

In the life after this test, where eternity awaits, you will be seized and judged with full force.

And as for us – we had removed ourselves from the Creator's gracious hand and paid more attention to others. We became dependent on the world.

And now we are empty-handed.

Now we have no more protection from the fire.

But hear us:

With body and soul we now hasten to the Creator's throne to ask Him for forgiveness.

He is our Creator, and we beg His assistance.

And even if we should perish now, we will not remain separate from Him!"

The fire laughed.

"Then die."

Ferociously and inexorably, the flames surrounded the few righteous men until a roar of thunder rang from the sky.

Together they looked up, startled and confused.

Gray clouds floated heavily and gloomily over them, and with the next rumble of thunder, rain burst upon the earth.

"Don't you know, arrogant fire, that everyone, good or bad, has a limited time in the kingdom of earth? Did you not know that you, too, will soon disappear from the world's stage? Then the Creator's just reward awaits you! Now know also that the Creator has an antidote for everything, and without directly intervening. So that He may remain hidden in the interest of the test, He punishes with the hand of His servants.

Now away with your pitiful entourage! Never come here again. Other bad influences will come. But they will leave also.

And you, you happy resisters, live free and contented again. But you are also to blame.

Deny evil from the very beginning, before it gains so much power that you can no longer resist it.

Behold!

Now you understand …" The fire went out with a crackling noise. "… that everything bad is weak.

Because nothing stands behind it."

The Sun

Once the sun was shining in the sky.
The people, and I too, thanked Allah for this gift and went about our work.
Then evening fell.
Suspicion and strife spread among the people.
Little by little, they became entangled in the addicting desire to be the strongest.
And the darker it got, the more desolate the earth looked.
And when the last rays of the sun departed, all the evildoers stepped out and saw the darkness as an opportunity to strike.
The sun had disappeared.
And people fought many battles.
Great confusion prevailed, and many souls suffered much.
A few good men joined forces.
They soon had a plan.
They wanted to bring back the sun so that the bad men would have to leave.
They went to where it had set and with ropes and cords tried to force the sun to come back.
I looked out the window, pulled aside the curtain, and expressionlessly tried to make sense of all the troubles, the mischief, the chaos.
A I found one single thing that made sense.
There was a lack of faith in the Creator.
Those who had believed in sunny times had now forgotten that belief, abandoned it, or set it aside in the many battles.
And that is why they could not defeat the bad men.
The fortunes of war merely passed back and forth.
I did not fight.
It was not yet time for that.

Soon I turned away from the combatants and looked toward the desperate ones who were trying to bring back the sun.
I knew how futile these efforts were.
For the sun followed its course.
Then I looked at the moon.
It shone a beautiful white.
I had a flash of inspiration.
The moon reflects the light of the sun.
So the sun was never gone.
It was always there.
The light was always there.
Only the sun had turned away from us.
And we ourselves were to blame.
Then I looked at the desperate people.
And I thought:
"You are looking for the sun where it set.
However, it will not rise there."
I whispered, "In the east … it is in the east that the sun rises."
I took a lantern and lit it.
So you can have light when you need it.
And soon, after the purification of the good, all the faithful held lanterns and now walked safely and resolutely toward the evil ones.
These latter were startled to see the bright light … and fled to their safe, dark hiding places.
The faithful cheered.
And thereupon they saw the light shining in the east.
The sun gave birth to pleasant, warming rays.
Even greater and more lasting was the joy that followed.
Tears were shed, laughter rose to heaven, and people thanked the Creator and went about their duties again.
I looked out at life beyond my window.
People had been created weak.
People were forgetful.
And there was good as well as bad in every person.

And those who hid their bad by day, even though it was greater than their good and completely obscured it, would soon strike again.

And then the darkness would fall again.

Was this our destiny, since the sun always sets and then rises again? No.

We humans are so predictable and transparent for the sun, and that is why it always knows in advance when to disappear and when to appear again for its reward.

That's how predictable man is. Our history proves it.

The Wall

There was a wall.
It was white and flat.
No cracks were visible on it.
And it was the only structure on a lush summer meadow.
Its outlines were even.
It was whole, although it must have fallen over at some point.
Why didn't you break into pieces upon that impact?
Or did they lay you here gently?
What is your purpose?
Is it the picture you bear?
That rests on you?
What did I see in the picture?
I saw something very impressive.
Something particularly important to me.
I will not tell you what I saw.
For the secret of this image is this:
Everyone sees something different in it.
There I stood in front of that picture.
It was crooked.
Then I straightened the large painting.
And it was finally right side up in front of me.
Suddenly a stranger was standing next to me, looking at me instructively.
"Can't you see that the picture is crooked?" He placed it so that it was in front of him.
"That's better."
Another figure appeared across from us. "What on earth are you doing?" And she moved the picture to face her.
The man drew a deep breath.
"You've turned the picture upside down!"

The woman shook her head. "No. I saved the painting from destruction."

All at once, a crowd of people stood huddled in a circle around the wall.

"There." – "No, this way." – "Stop! This is the way!"

People tugged and pulled at the picture.

Everyone was trying to help.

But they wanted to help in a way that fit their point of view.

I stood motionless, watching silently.

I felt as though I saw suffering in that picture.

Its honor, its pride, the greatness of the painting, where had they gone?

Quickly, before we disgraced ourselves, I plucked the picture out of the mayhem.

Now we were all frozen.

It took time for us to understand.

For too long, our thoughts had been focused on one thing.

Although I still held the picture, motionless, everyone stood up straight.

No one said anything.

I pointed to the picture.

"The picture is what it is no matter which way you turn it."

A figure spoke.

"If we put the wall up, it would be oriented correctly."

I did not speak immediately, but waited.

"We're going to have a hard time getting this picture right. Because everyone will think only of themselves and those standing with them when they try to straighten it."

"So what is right?" someone asked.

"Let's place it on our heart and make it our crown. Then it won't matter which way the picture is turned, will it?"

The crowd was not yet satisfied.

"But we know how to do it right."

Together they erected the wall and hung the picture straight.

They looked at it as if spellbound.

Some thought the picture was too far away, too close, too far left, too far right.

Others already understood. They looked at the picture with warmth and love.

Many have seen more pictures, and more beautiful ones, since.

And before I left, I thought, "Don't try to orient the picture to you – orient yourself to the picture."

The Raging Torrent

I saw it today: I am in a raging torrent.
I am being carried away.
And I am letting myself be carried away.
I try to do everything just right.
It is not easy.
And it is crushing to see that soon, if I find no way out, I myself will become part of that raging torrent.
I should avoid particularly dangerous rapids and use shallower places.
And I see through the rushing water:
Everyone presents himself.
They may feel ugly, beautiful, weak, or strong.
That water says, I am superior. Muddy water stays at the bottom and does not like to rise.
Doesn't the water want to be united?
Distrusting itself, it swirls and flows, leaps and caresses, glides and floats and lashes out.
Water, I beg you! You diminish me. You confuse me. You silence me.
Around me that restlessness, in me that rabidness. I am losing myself.
Tell me, water, am I living?
Or am I being guided by external forces?
Everything flows, water. Everything goes in one direction, water. And everything is content with that, water.
Tell me, water, will you let me go again?
Why not? Explain yourself.
Would others want to follow?
Are you going to drown me now?
Believe, water, that if the Lord left me alone again, I would again try to find a way out of here.
For I no longer wish to be your water.

I want to be a dewdrop, I want to be vapor, I no longer want to
be here with you.
But this is how I can see that even then I am controlled from
the outside.
The sun's heat moves to leave you, the shore's will holds me. I
should leave you, lured by the blossom and enticed never to leave it.
Tell me, water, where shall I go?
Where can I turn?
And I tell you this, stream of water:
If I am not to be left alone without someone else steering me, I
want to be steered by the greatest of all steersmen.
The flower is controlled by earth, water, sun, and seasons.
The sun is controlled by the universe.
And the universe?
Not just the universe, flowing stream, but you, too?
And everything else, visible and invisible?
Everything is controlled by the Creator, wild river.
And even if I let myself be controlled, voluntarily or not, it will
be for the Lord.
The direction in which I flow may be the wrong one.
But then I will stay on the periphery if I can't get away from you.
And who knows, maybe I will reach a more peaceful land.
Maybe someday I will get to float.
I will wait, river.
There is nothing else for me to do.
And one day, river, it will be time.
I believe it.
With all my heart.
For the Creator is great.
My journey so far has been long.
We will see where it leads us.
And listen: If I don't get away from you, can we end up as a little
stream or flow into the deep sea?
All our journeys are uncertain.
Yet we don't realize that every drop of water contributes to us
being who we are.

Do You Promise Me That?

"All is well.
I am happy.
And I don't even realize that I'm happy.
All is well and going in the right direction.
I hope everything will always stay that way."

All at once, dark clouds gather.
Suffering.
More suffering.
More pain.
Gradually the shoulders droop.
Impotence builds in the face of the unbearable and the scorching.
All at once, everything becomes dark.
What now? Where to turn? When more and more doors close in front of you? Just give up? Admit defeat in the face of a life that longer wants what you want?
And in the distance, a glimmer appears in the gloom. It takes shape and form, and all at once, stands before you like a little star. Drenched in suffering, you look to the light.
Anger boils up inside you. You do not want to see it.
"Go away! I don't want you! Why have you come, now that I have lost everything good? Why do you come, now that I stand alone in this place, without refuge, exposed by existence? What do you want from me now? To taunt me with the illusion of courage? To appease me? No! I don't need you! You abandoned me! Away! Away with you!"
You are writhing in pain and sorrowfully bow your head.
"Neither you nor your kind. I do not want you."
The light is silent and warms you again and again.
The light is silent and loves you more and more.

You come to yourself and inhale.

You lean back against the wall, and warm tears trace radiant lines down your face.

The light expands, filling the whole room.

Quietly it begins to speak, and a wonderful feeling of well-being spreads in your breast.

"Your tests are difficult, dearest child.

Your burden is heavy now after blissful times.

But you are not alone.

The angels in the firmament suffer with you and weep because of your great burden.

But the way to the Lord is not far.

Do not give up, child of heaven.

Don't let your reins fall.

Fight to the end.

Promise me that.

Will you fight, with yourself and the world, for the Creator of worlds, to the end?

Do you promise?

Will you fight in life as long as your strength lasts and not give up?

Do you promise?

That you will then gloriously enter eternity, no matter what the world says?

That you will keep going, no matter how bad things get?

That you will believe in yourself and the Creator, no matter how the world sees you?

Then arise, my child, and henceforth realize that you are the Lord's treasure and will receive great homage in the true kingdom.

But you still have to learn this: Believe that absolutely everything will be all right. And pray to your Lord to save you and deliver you from this gloom. You must sincerely ask your Creator and firmly hold to your desire, aligning yourself with it.

And now come, start towards the light.

I will always be your companion."

And you stand up and smile brightly.

And hand in hand you walk with the light through the world.
The darkness moves aside a little with every step, and the light
fills you now, inside and out.

How the Pearl Changes

A sea lies before us.

A bad area surrounds it.

We have constant dangers to deal with.

This is how it appears when we take a quick look around.

"Let's not pay attention to it today," we think.

And so we stand and examine the sea more closely.

Its beautiful turquoise color sparkles at us.

What could be beautiful there when the surroundings seem so gloomy?

But we surrender to the inner urge and approach the water.

It warms our feet.

But that's as far as anyone wants to go.

Are there no brave ones among us?

One person screws up his courage and rushes into the water.

For a long time, we wait for him to appear again.

Some want to swim after him, but then he reappears.

But he is changed.

Purified, it appears to us.

And he exclaims, "I wouldn't have guessed it, but it's beautiful down there!" And he holds something up in the air: a large pearl. He is delighted and says, "At first it was so dark, but I did not give up. I dived even deeper. I wanted to unravel the mystery of this gloom and why the sea had so suddenly become dark. And when I was almost ready to turn back, things around me became brighter. The further I went, the more beautiful and brighter things became. And as I enchantedly absorbed all these impressions, I noticed a glimmer. My lungs, which had been bursting, suddenly relaxed. I swam towards the glimmer and saw a pearl in a seashell. I rejoiced and almost flew to it. When I touched that pearl, it spoke to me."

"What did it say?" we asked.

He lifted the pearl. "Put your hands on it."
We did as he said. And a voice said, "The truth is as hard to reach
as I am." And the pearl shone and took on a different form.
It became a holy book.
We were astonished, but our hearts began to understand.
And we had questions.
Then a stranger came along.
He said, "That book will answer all your questions."
We opened it. And the book's first warning was not to be among
those who go astray on earth.
Then someone said, "These here have gone astray."
And the person holding the Holy Book smiled strangely and spoke:
"The question is who has gone astray, and whether any righteous
are left at all."
"What should we do?"
He lifted the Holy Book. "If we follow Him, everything will be
fine. Whoever wants to can come with me."
And slowly we moved forward, and the calmness in our eyes
sends out a clear message:
Wait for us.
We have time.
And follow us.
We are ready.

The Downfall

At a time when horses still pulled the wagons and fire burned in fireplaces, a young man was struggling through his life.
The people to whom he belonged went about their daily work, at times sacrificing particularly handsome animals to the gods.
But the peace was disturbed by a middle-aged man.
He preached to gatherings of people about one God, claiming that he was a prophet, the messenger of that God.
The young man watched the behavior of the village elders.
They threatened the preacher and mocked him.
So the young man assumed that such behavior was appropriate.
He, too, laughed at the preacher and whistled loudly.
Even the poor poet or magician heard him and looked briefly in his direction.
"From time immemorial, we have believed and held fast to our faith. You will not be able to change it," said the elders.
Unwaveringly, the preacher talked to the bystanders. He said that he asked for no reward or any worldly goods. He wanted only to save people from eternal punishment in the name of the Creator.
For days, the young man saw how he labored to convince people.
It was not that preacher did not impress him, but that he represented danger.
Something had to be done about that.
There would otherwise be a disturbance among the gods.
And a god? Perfect? A life after death? Death and resurrection? Heaven and hell?
It was as if someone were grabbing his heart.
Filled with pain, he tensed.
"He is a magician. He is trying to cast a spell on me.
The elders of our people have a better idea of what is right and good.
Our faith is the true faith.

There can be nothing else."
And one day, as the preacher spoke, more and more voices were raised at him.
"Let your God send us punishment!"
"We are ready. What comes will come!"
"Go ahead, do your worst!"
"Then we will believe him."
An unspeakable pain appeared on the prophet's face. He was silent at first, then spoke for the last time.
"You will get what you want."
There was silence. Then the first responses came:
"He is a sorcerer. Leave him!" And they left him.
The following day, the young man saw how the prophet and his few followers were packing to go and leave the unspeakable people, as they called them, to their fate.
And after they left, the world rumbled.
In a panic, the citizens of the city ran around in confusion.
The young man was paralyzed.
"Does he exist after all, this one God?"
And a scream rent the air.
And left behind only ashes.
This was the punishment for those who deny the Creator and His messengers.

The Strange Game

Let's play a dice game.
And the pieces will stand for people.
The die is cast.
It is the first piece's move.
But it does not budge.
It insistently remains where it is.
It thinks, "Here I stand and am not at liberty to go further. That which is now is good."
Then it is the next piece's turn.
It pays no attention to the number on the die and chooses a square to advance to at random.
"I follow my own laws," it says.
Then the next piece takes its turn.
It goes twice as far as the number on the die.
"I deserve better," it says.
Then the next piece takes its turn.
It thinks, "What right does the cube have to determine my path? I'll choose my own way." And it chooses its own square.
Then the next piece takes its turn.
The stone is warped. It trembles while the die rolls, and as soon as the number comes into view, it dashes off and sits on the right-hand square.
Then the next piece takes its turn.
It goes one space, then two, and then lies on its side.
"I've done enough for today," it says.
Then the next piece takes its turn.
It says: "This board is a coincidence. It has come into being on its own. And I will do what I want in my time on it."
Then the next piece takes its turn.
It says, "I live only once. So I should enjoy life. My life revolves around fun."

And it bounces up and down on its square.

Then the next piece takes its turn.

It jumps on the square and pushes some pieces out of the square and off the table.

"I do bad things and no one punishes me. And I like being an evildoer."

Then the next piece takes its turn. It stands in the middle of the game, calling out to the other stones, "This game is outdated. Let's think of new, better ones."

There is great chaos. But the game goes on.

A piece notices this condition and finds it regrettable.

It is now its turn.

It asks, "Why should I play this game?"

The answer comes: "To reach the destination."

"What awaits me at the destination?"

"The eternal reward of your Creator."

"But no one follows that path sincerely or knows why he is following it. Why do you not stop the game?"

"We wait until every stone has had its turn."

"And then?"

"Then every stone gets its reward based on what it has accomplished."

The piece nods.

"Then I will follow this path for the Creator."

The Shadow

She said, "Shadow that runs before me, you are so unreachable.
I see you, you hurry ahead of me and no matter how fast I run, you always remain in front of me.
You're smothering me and you don't realize it.
You neither anticipate nor account for my effort.
You are indifferent and do not see my needs.
You flow away, and no power on earth will let me reach you.
I run impetuously after you, and you just laugh.
So I stop and look at you.
Wearily I sit down on the ground and withstand your gaze.
And I think to myself:
Shadow that rests before me, you expect so much.
Today you are superior to me.
But tomorrow you will be behind me, and I will forget the effort I made to reach you.
For tomorrow I will know more and see more clearly."
And she ran over hill and dale, through storm and snow, crossed mountain and valley.
And one day she noticed something as she walked … and she turned around.
The shadow was now behind her.
And she laughed.
She spun around on her toes.
Not taking her eyes off the shadow, she thought:
"Now look, shadow.
You've been laughing constantly. Was this because of my simplicity?
Now I realize that only when a person frees himself from expectations will he be able to see again.
My blinders were a great burden that I found difficult to bear.
And now that I see you better, you are always at my feet.

My plans and goals, which I thought up for myself, are not righteous. They only constrain me.

Today I will run after my heart and not despair.

To avoid despair, follow your heart.

For in the heart rests the Creator.

He will show you the right way.

And, shadow that accompanies me, one day I want to learn why you were always laughing."

Immediately a whisper played around her ears, saying, "Your efforts to do what is right make me laugh.

And my struggles to follow your meandering haste make me laugh.

And knowing that your compass was resting inside you and that you didn't realize it made me laugh.

But now you understand, and that makes me laugh.

I love you. Because you love what is good.

The Creator surrounds us. That makes me laugh.

And now just keep on until your path ends. I will always be your companion.

Then the actual journey towards eternity began in peace.

Up There

For a long time, I have been working to climb these high stairs. I stand, looking around me, sometimes hesitating, sometimes accusing myself, sometimes feeling sorry for myself, sometimes losing my bearings – and all the while a thousand spirits try to seduce and beguile me.

"Leave your path. It is much more pleasant with us. You will enjoy yourself and have the best experiences," they say.

The spirits then pull me back, trying with all their might to get me to leave the stairs and join them and let myself drift in life.

Then I look around.

I have come a fair way, of course.

But the way back seems so much easier than the way up.

And doubts arise.

What if I reach the heights and then fall?

What if I lose?

Oh dear. A doubt. But you do not disturb me. The thousand spirits would not get me down from here.

Don't you know, doubt, that I started far below? That I have lost so many times in life?

Now just watch me get up there.

There will be no stopping. All I want is to get up there.

You see, I will fight.

I will just keep fighting and fighting – even you won't stop me.

Why aren't you laughing anymore?

Are you going to change strategy and attack?

Here they come, the spirits of the world, trying to ensnare me – if they didn't stop me like that, would they use more severe weapons come?

Now you are clinging to me? Do you want to pull me down from the steps, block my path with all the means available to you? Well then, cling to me.

I will climb the stairs.
If you do not let me go, I would pull you along and carry you.
A thousand spirits, I will drag you along.
A thousand weights pressing on me, I will learn to carry you.
A thousand spirits, a thousand weights, will you not leave me?
Then come along.
With or without the world's blessing, I am going up there.
Because of the burdens and a thousandfold distractions, my head
has always been bowed.
For they don't want to see me make it up there.
I'm swimming against the current to get there.
But I no longer see anything else.
Up there.
And when I get there?
Then I found ways to say: Further, always further up there!
Do not stop me.
And if my path were to end?
I would come back, I would come back to say, Up there!

The Sea

Look, how tempting the wide sea is.
How its charms lure and draw me to it.
Don't I want to let myself fall into it? And lose my orientation and my senses?
So that the waves may flow around me in the melody of the endless expanses?
I got in and drank of the divine wine, so that I forgot where I had came from and where my path was leading me.
Everything was quiet, and I drifted drunkenly in the gentle water.
I saw the sky above me and how eternity surrounded and filled me.
A thousand gentle waves swept past me and passed their melody on to me. In the midst of the noise, I forgot who I was, where I had come from, and where my path led. Everything was silent.
That mighty place contained nothing and everything.

But my friend, how quickly this paradise can change.
How quickly storm clouds can gather and make me tremble.
It was serene and heavenly and I came to my senses, inhaling deeply, letting my self return home to its earthly shell, thanking Allah for his precious gift. I pulled myself from the sea once again.
On the shore, I gazed warmly at the endless expanses.
This is the world, great sea.
If I let myself fall completely, it would shake me mercilessly.
The world imposes my duties on me, and I want to perform them with a clear conscience.
And if a sweet whisper were to arise again, I would let myself fall again and sink to you.
To then open my eyes again and go about my duties.
My heart draws me to you.
But the world says that I have many duties.
So I am patient and live as long as I have breath.

And we humans must work in order to live.
A beautiful consolation are the seconds in You as we dive into
the world of endlessness and glory.
There are so many ways to reach you.
As long as the ways are righteous, the heart drinks its nourish-
ment: the light of the Lord Almighty.

Not Them

A big waterfall is what I see now.
But it is not what moves me.
A beautiful river is what shows itself to me now.
But it is not what moves me.
A wise sea is what appears before me.
But it is not what is near me.
A deep ocean is what reveals itself to me.
But it is not what purifies me.
A lovely brook is what splashes before me.
But it is not what reaches me.
And I see a trickle come out of the eye of the bowed, the mourned, the grieved, the pained.
This I kiss the tear, pressing it to me.
This is what touches me.
This is what I love.
This is what I care about.
Do not cry.
There is someone who remains with you.
Even if the world leers at and mocks you, someone is with you.
As terrible as everything may suddenly seem, someone will always be with you.
And if everything were to lose its value, someone would remain unaffected.
And if you are hurt and nevertheless burdened with even more – someone will care for you.
I will take you by the hand.
The Creator is with you.
He knows about you.
He is the only One.
He loves you.
Go to Him.

Let all the thinking, feeling, speaking, and acting do as it will.
Just let the Creator touch you.
So that everything else must yield.
And now fly and float through your feelings and continue through your life – it is no longer able to defeat you.

Love You

Often a person is unhappy in his own body.

The are various reasons for this.

They can be too ugly, too unsuccessful, too weak, and much more.

Do you take yourself to task, blame yourself? Are you even at war with yourself?

You don't see how beautiful and perfect you are at heart.

And you don't realize that everything is good the way it is.

Won't you realize that you, your body, your mind, and your soul serve you eternally and accompany you wherever you go?

That your self is always trying to support you in the best way possible in everything?

Don't you see how pure your innermost being fundamentally is, whether the world recognizes it or not?

The Creator sees it.

You see it.

What more do you need?

With the Creator behind you and you yourself as your greatest refuge, you need no more.

You will remain strong all your life.

You have been beautiful since the beginning of time.

And you will conquer the world. You are a rock that can withstand the waves of the ocean.

You will not sink again.

The Creator and you.

What more do you need?

So say, here and now, that you love yourself.

And realize, here and now, that the Creator and you are your best medicine and that you will never give up.

You will begin to lift your head from the trap.

And you will start to fight.
For good, for life, and for eternity.
Giving up is out of the question, my good friend.
The power of your soul is enough for eternity.

The Hasty Old Man

A stooped old man was always on the run.

All his life he hurried, rushing ahead.

He ran and ran. "Just leave me alone," he shouted.

His suffering was excessive, and he did not admit to himself that he was running away from himself. He dared not look inside himself. He did not like to see what was there.

"I've aged so much," he thought to himself.

"But nothing I do is right.

How am I to stand still, and how am I to persist when there is nothing I do well and enjoy doing?"

He ran and ran. "I will run until the end," he said to himself, until he tripped over a stone lying on the path.

He fell heavily, and his knee pained him terribly.

He paused for a moment and took a breath.

He saw in amazement that many were running.

He looked and looked and murmured and listened to what was going on around him.

He watched them running, and his face stiffened.

"Did I really look like that?"

Amazed, he kept watching.

He saw the quiet woods and the bustling nearby city and soon realized something:

"I see that I have to get over it."

He stood up briskly and shook the dust from his clothes. Once again he wiped his shoulder.

He slapped it, thinking cheerfully:

"You walk all your life, and a small stone brings you down.

Why did you not go your way calmly and circumspectly?

I was afraid to look myself in the eyes, but it was with those eyes that I was looking for a way out.

Now I laugh and just say:

From now on, I will silently fathom my inmost being and overcome my fear of my weakness.
For running without a goal is a never-ending game, and you
never leave the beginning of your path."

The Wisdom of Trees

Now I am looking at a tree in late summer, almost the beginning of autumn.

"Strange tree," I think.

"There you have labored all spring and summer to grow your leaves, your foliage, and now that it is ripe you will soon part with it. Grow and release. Grow and release. Grow and release.

What wisdom does this behavior conceal?

Grow and release.

Draw the air into yourself and be convinced that wisdom is hidden in everything. That everything bears Allah's signature.

The tree then sheds its leaves when it knows that they are complete. And gives them to those who need them more than it does.

It will remember this ripeness forever, but does not keep it to itself. It hands this ripeness over to others.

Because it now wants to devote itself to new ripeness. And it will give that ripeness away also.

If it were selfish and did not want others to share in its work and possessions, what would happen?

Perhaps then it would no longer be able to grow new leaves, and the ones it had would rot and make the tree sick.

Or, over the years, so many leaves would grow on it that it would eventually break from the weight.

What does this mean?

Learn. Then give. Then work. And give away the harvest. Then educate yourself properly. And let go of what has grown and let it go its way. Then reflect. And leave the harvest to your neighbors.

Do not desire.

No.

Give and give and give."

Do You Love?

Whatever or whomever.
Do you love?
Do you deny this feeling?
Are you trying to hide from it?
Don't you want to accept this invitation?
Do you love?
Are you afraid of the wide gates that lead to an unknown, uncertain, misunderstood world?
Are a thousand spirits plucking at your reason and your mind, telling you to get away?
But how far are you going to run?
Do you love?
They all say: Love everything and everyone.
How is that supposed to work?
Do you love?
Tell me, do you love?
Out with it! Do you love?
Don't love everyone right away, bitter little friend, just love first.
It should be pure.
Free and happy.
First love honestly and without encumbrance.
Do you think this is the sprout?
Tell me, here and now: Do you love?

What I Want

I long for the good, beautiful things in life.
I long for the Creator, the pure good.
All good, perfect qualities are His.
Everything defective, imperfect, and inadequate is far from Him.
I always carry the Creator in my heart.
I thus also always carry the good in my heart.
I love the Creator.
And I love the good.
It is for the Creator alone that I long.
I ask the Creator alone for assistance.
To the Creator alone I aspire.
For the Creator, I have gladly fought alongside the good worldwide for the victory of good on earth since the beginning of time.
I want it.
I want to be among those who fought for the victory of good.
And I want to testify in their memory that even today there are those who strive for the good and can look down on us with reassurance and pride.
Those who are good do not capitulate.
Because the Creator is the goal.
For Him we gladly suffer, love, and fight.

Hidden Heroes

There are heroes on earth.
Even today.
But you do not see them or recognize them.
You will also never understand what they do and how they do it.
For this is one of the secrets of the Lord of the worlds.
They work and toil unswervingly. No mind can ever grasp their endless passion.
You will never see them exhausted.
If they were to fall, you would realize that they had reached their limits.
They do not burn.
They are already fire.
Instead, they burn what they touch.
They do not suffer. They go on the offensive.
You want to instruct them?
They just laugh and remain silent.
For that which instructs them is something you do not see.
They carry this world, you know?
You don't see them. They walk with the shadows.
The world should exert its influence.
They take care of its existence.
There are hidden heroes on earth.

The Snowman

A snowman in wind, snow, and storm defies all circumstances
and fate until he disappears.
He doesn't even know why he is defiant.
For he has no inner life.
His life is what you see on the outside.
Does he therefore have value?
Does he get excited and then just disappear?
Snowman, I like you very much.
Your presence is a comfort and blessing.
And yet you never do anything.
You are what they wanted you to be.
That's how you were formed.
And you never fought back.
Snowman, snowman, you let everything influence you.
The one who forms you, builds you; the environment, the climate, the circumstances; the snowmen who were before you,
those who you think have told you what a snowman is.
Snowman, snowman, you let everything influence you except
yourself.
Why do you exist?
Tell me, snowman, is it bad if people just forget about you?

The Snail

Snail, I see so many laugh at you.
They say that you are too slow and make little progress.
And yet the Creator created you with purpose and value.
Snail, you carry your house with you no matter where you are.
You don't need to run or hide.
If you see danger, you retreat into your house.
And, snail, your house is made from your flesh and blood. It is just right for what you need.
You say, "When you have no reason to rush and can survive anywhere, you seem to those who rush and make noise like someone from another world."
I'm going with you, snail.
Let those who don't understand laugh. You are proof that survival without rushing is possible.
You are precious and valuable to me.
You do not know how grateful I am to you.
And it is possible that my flesh and blood will one day become a house, because our genes are not dissimilar.

The Light

The sun has already disappeared. But for a while the light remains, breathed in by my heart and absorbed by my eyes, until the last beautiful gleam is gone.

But the sun with its warm, comforting rays remains and does not leave.

For it is in me. It became a part of me long ago.

Still, although in deep night, I feel the maternal embrace of the rays, the paternal protection of warmth, and the lovely, tender, deeply touching gold. It is still there.

And it will not leave my side if I do not let it. As long as I don't let this piece of paradise be taken away from me by ravens, crows, rats, hyenas, snakes, and pigs. As long as I don't let it break me. Because these rays belong to me. No one can grasp them with his hand and steal them from me, dispute them with me, or tear them from me. No. The light is in me, it belongs to me.

I love it. And it returns my love. So I am safe. Safe and sound in the dungeon without light. But who cares about that? I myself am light.

And I believe that the light will once again free me from darkness and lead me to daylight.

Encouragement

Do not despair. You will make it one day. You will break the chains of this world one day. Don't look around so bitterly. Your life will soon be worth living again. Do not grieve for the past. You will save today. Do not sink in your worries. You will free yourself from them. Do not mourn your mistakes. You will leave them behind.

Open your eyes carefully and look around. Can't you see how beautiful the world is? The Creator made it for you and me. He gave us our suffering, it is true, but He also gave us love, joy, bliss, and security. Shouldn't we taste both the bad and the good in order to mature?

I tell you this, my friend. I may sink into darkness and never find my way out, I may burn in flames and become ashes, but my faith in the Creator will endure. So I will never be alone, even if the whole world wars against me. No. My faith will remain no matter how flawed I am, no matter how weak I am, and no matter how much I suffer. Faith will endure. And I believe that one day this faith will free me from the darkness.

The Wonderland

Are you looking for wonderland on earth? Where there is no sorrow? Where there is no suffering? Where there is no pain? Where there are no tears?
Then come with me on my journey, friend.
For I, too, seek that place.
I look for it day and night.
But that place will appear only when you yourself begin to heal.
If you improve carefully.
When you look around and give the world a pure smile and convert it.
Tell those sorrowful people that there is a wonderland.
They should follow you and accompany you.
And one day we will find it.
For the wonderland gives birth to each individual for himself.
It is hidden.
In your heart.
Come on, bring it out.
Perhaps the realm of your soul is more beautiful than mine.
So open up.
And teach me.

Allow Miracles

Open up.
Experience miracles again.
For miracles surround you, even if you close yourself off from them. You alone have closed your gates to them, so that they can no longer visit you.
What you believe is not absolute reality, but only a small part of it. It comes to you through the open gates of that which you believe.

Faith opens the gates of sublimity.
And only the sublime knows how many gates and secrets sublimity and omnipotence provide to each person.

The Lonely Tree

I walk through the streets of this city,
Which has nothing but many people.
Tired, I return to my comforting home,
Look out the window, see just a tree.

Its relatives are far away, its family gone,
It is still standing upright in this gray, noisy place.
Wistfully and sadly I keep it company.
"I am strong," it murmurs softly and virtuously.

It breathes the exhaust fumes of the many cars.
It tells me, "This is my home."
Its branches are pruned and ordered,
So that it does not cause trouble or present an obstacle.

"Where did you get such patience and strength?"
I asked him admiringly.
"I trust in Allah and his imminent reward
And my pride, as I undergo my great test."

And I say, "It is the same with people,
For each of us, a different test strives to prevail.
Don't you think Allah called this world a place of testing?
To determine who will inhabit the heavens?

Allah has ranked us through our work
And waits to see what we will do on earth.
Do you think good and bad have equal value?
Some deserve heaven, others hell's hearth."

The tree laughs heavily and sublimely at me,
"Don't you know that you are like me?"
Confused, I look up and ask:
"Am I really? Then I would be very rich."

The tree is still silent and smiles warmly.
"Do you realize now that people are poor?
They see only what they must see,
they hear only what they must hear.

Hardly anyone really sees me anyway
And if they do, they are not particularly cordial.
And as for you, my child,
You are different from many people.

We are related because we love the Lord
And we suffer gladly for His grace and presence."

Monologue

Sluggishly I pull myself forward,
When was the last time I didn't long for rest?
I do not understand the world in its haste,
It will eventually break my heart.

I can rarely be as I really am,
I can often not be how I want to be.
I just keep going in the same circles,
What an incredibly long journey.

Everything often seems pointless to me,
I never felt weightless.
I was allowed to feel only this miserable burden,
I have hated nothing else so thoroughly.

I am rarely satisfied with what I do,
I demand too much, can't rest.
My thoughts do not allow it,
They are not to be believed.

I often want to live alone forever,
With no one to ever disturb my being.
No one to distract me,
Nothing to seduce me.

Of course I may see only blackness,
But then nothing remains in my heart.
The more I come to know,
The more a cosmos, full of warning, opens up to me.

It tells me to be very careful,
What you want to achieve is difficult.
And never lose your true purpose,
There is a fine line between genius and madness.

Love

I saw in the deep, dark glow
Of the cloudy night
A breathtaking dance
Of two with fervent power.

They swirled with urgency and melody,
They danced with abandon and excess,
They roared along the land,
To an unfathomable, perpetual extent.

These two have danced since the beginning of time
And yet – they remained unrecognized forever.
The love that inspired them was elemental and vast
Like the sky above them, an endless place.

And forever they would dance and float
And always touch people on their journey,
So that their love is inflamed with blessings,
So that they embrace the great feeling in their hearts.

The paths of the dancing couple were uncertain,
Inexplicable were their goals and intentions,
Do not ask why and wherefore – you do not know,
The lovers, were they afraid of heavy loads?

And yet – tirelessly the dancing truth swirled,
And the dancing couple did not ask whether they felt ready.
The labyrinth of love was certainly a myth without equal,
For experiencing great things, sent by a god.

Realm of the Soul

I sing and play, freely and without burden,
I know no rest or peace.
I search and discern at my discretion,
Minor worries are already forgotten.

A whirlwind arises from the realm of my soul,
It wants to carry me into my realm,
My realm is full of the most precious things,
I salute every masterpiece.

My treasure is not of jewels or gold,
The written word is my fair home.
I honor the works of bright senses so great,
Wisdom, knowledge, insight, that is my lot.

I sometimes wander the forest,
Suffer wounds now and again.
Off to my safe kingdom
Where the treasures heal quickly, so I am rich.

My Islam

I have one wish,
That many people love you
And no longer hurt you,
O my Islam.

I have but one request,
That we would become Muslims again
And not ally ourselves with frustration,
O my Islam.

I call out one word,
To end all evil,
Allah is our course,
O my Islam.

One name I proclaim,
Who has always guided you and me,
"Mohammed", Allah exalt you,
O my Islam.

That's all it takes,
For they form a weight,
That forces everything down,
O my Islam.

The young boy

The young boy quietly sings,
Thanking the Lord for His gift,
All that he received perpetually,
Health, happiness, and bread.

He sings louder now and smiles,
The good heart he has
Be to him an exalted treasure,
The virtue, warmth, and generosity.

Up and down the notes flow,
What is commanded on earth,
How beautiful the world is,
The meadows are a lovely place.

The boy bows down,
All our paths are eternal,
We soon will meet again,
In the hereafter, in eternity, in life.

Rest

Running on puddles of water I come,
The wind blows my cloak away from far off.
I watch the sunset in silence,
See the thunderclouds twitching as they display their lightning.

Wrap myself slowly in darkness,
Keep silence in solitude.
Enjoying this soundless peace,
Is like flowing with the river.

Again I sink into my thoughts,
Observe nature and can only give thanks.
My gaze wanders to the starry sky
And finds an answer in all the hustle and bustle.

I am in company, although I am alone,
After all, there are friends of solitude everywhere.
We feel each other's presence without seeing each other,
The same thing is probably true of the stars.

The Power That Rests Within Me

Here is my heart,
Do you see it?
It endures much pain,
Do you believe it?
Mark this heart well, my friend,
So far it has not shied away from anyone.
Look at it, never forget it,
It will bring all opponents to their knees.
Take your whip and strike about you, frighten me,
Offer me riches, say what you want in return.
This body would stand behind you immediately,
But that piece of flesh will survive both you and me.
Tell me, poor enemy that you are,
What good is all your cunning?

Love

I love to love.
Love makes me forget death.
I love to die.
The agony makes me forget about life.
And I love
To listen to you, beloved.
Your presence,
Even if you remain silent,
Makes me forget the world.

May Kuvvet eternally follow her path and find happiness.
And may her search for truth and wisdom last a lifetime.
Her goal is to better understand the Creator and His work.
And therefore herself.
And all her efforts are directed toward this principle:
Believe in what you want – but choose the good.
Strive for the good, virtuous perfection, and flee evil and error.
Strive.
Let it be your purpose in life. Seek perfection, enlightenment, wisdom.
And perfection has many names.
And this message has been drawn out for understanding minds.
And never forget: firmly believe that everything will be truly good in the end.

The author

Pinar Akdag was born in 1983. She received her
vocational baccalaureate diploma, completed her
training as a pharmaceutical technical assistant,
and began professional practice. But she could
never identify with the work, so she devoted
herself to writing.

She started writing fifteen years ago, and four
years ago made this passion her profession. Today
she is a freelance author and copywriter. Her works
have been published by various houses, including
her new book, "Wisdom from the heart", which
illustrates her love for storytelling and writing.